DEAD MAN'S NOOSE

DEAD MAN'S NOOSE

MORGAN HILL

Sage River Books *Sisters, Oregon*

DEAD MAN'S NOOSE
published by Sage River Books
© 2003 by ALJO PRODUCTIONS, INC.

International Standard Book Number: 1-59052- 277-X

Cover illustration © 2003 by Rene Milot. All rights reserved.

Printed in the United States of America

For information:
Sage River Books, Post Office Box 1720, Sisters, Oregon 97759

Library of Congress Cataloging-in-Publication Data

Hill, Morgan, 1933-
    Dead man's noose / by Morgan Hill.
        p. cm.
    ISBN 1-59052-277-X
    1. Sheriffs--Fiction. 2. Prisoners--Fiction. I. Title.
    PS3562.A256D43 2003
    813' .54--dc21

                                                        2003007816

        05 06 07 08 09 — 10 9 8 7 6 5 4 3 2 1

CHAPTER ONE

The afternoon sun slammed its merciless heat on the two riders. A lone buzzard eyed them from its lofty perch on the limb of a dead tree. The shimmering heat waves on the eastern horizon gave silent warning of the blistering torture that lay ahead.

One rider had an empty holster on his hip. His wrists, resting on the pommel of his saddle, were laced together with a rope. The other rider wore a star.

A pack horse followed, bearing sacks of grain and two large oak casks of water.

Sheriff Matt Blake had got his man at last. The seemingly endless manhunt climaxed in Yuma. There, Duke McClain had walked into a well-laid trap. Now he was being taken back to Tucson where a judge and a jury were waiting.

"You may put a rope on my wrists, Blake," McClain had said after he was caught, "but you'll never put one on my neck." Matt Blake had cinched the knot with a jerk. "I promise you, Mr. Lawman, you'll never get me to Tucson."

"We'll see."

"There's over two hundred miles of desert out there, Sheriff. A lot can happen."

"Shut up. Get on your horse," Blake had ordered.

That was over seven hours ago. They rode side by side, silently cursing the relentless sun. Dust climbed around them. Each man was alone with his thoughts.

The stretch of Arizona desert between Yuma and Tucson was a land of little water and less rain, where trails were marked by the sun-bleached bones of men and beasts that had died beside them. Getting across such rough territory was more a matter of having enough water than picking the shortest route. That was the first rule everybody learned.

Only six months before the Stillman Coach Lines had opened a stagecoach line between Tucson and Yuma. Coming out of Tucson, the stage would veer northward to the way station at Eloy, a distance of some fifty mile. A fresh team of horses would then carry the stage through sixty-five miles of heat and dust to Gila Bend. It was here the stage stopped for the night.

Heading to the southwest out of Gila Bend on the morning of the second day, the fresh team would haul the spinning wheels of the stagecoach along the banks of the Gila River. One more way station at Marquez Crossing provided a team of horses for the final fifty-mile stretch into Yuma. The need for fresh horses and the desperate need for water had established this roundabout route. Because of the heat, it was a full two days' journey.

Sheriff Matt Blake was not about to chance taking his prisoner in the stage, for even a man like McClain had friends. And McClain's friends were just as bad as he was. They wouldn't think twice about hitting the stage or even killing innocent passengers who got in the way. No, the only safe thing to do was to risk a nearly straight-line trip between Yuma and Tucson. Figuring to cover about thirty-five to forty miles a day, they would reach Tucson within six to seven days.

With the oak casks borne by the pack horse, and four canteens, the desert-wise lawman was satisfied there was sufficient water. Having made the same trip seven years before, Blake was familiar with what lay ahead. By keeping water consumption at a bare minimum and replenishing their supply at the water holes, the men and their horses weren't likely to die of thirst. This, Blake knew, was barring Indian trouble or other unforeseen events. The outlaw had been right about that—a lot can happen in two hundred miles of desert.

They must go easy on the horses, not push them too hard. Sheriff Blake was mounted on a zebra dun. He'd gone by stagecoach to Yuma and bought the dun and the gray roan pack horse from the local hostler for the return trip. The dun was a powerful horse with lightning speed. It was able to get along on less water than the other two horses.

The outlaw was mounted on his own bay. The gelding had not been bred for this kind of travel. It had never been called upon to bear this kind of heat on a minimum of water. The tall lawman was keenly aware that all three horses must be paced carefully. For without his horse, a man could not survive in this vast expanse of dust, sand, and heat. That was rule number two.

Then there were the water holes. Rule number three— don't miss 'em. Ahead of them, at least forty miles, was the first one. It lay in the shadow of a giant rock which resembled the head and profile of an Indian. To Blake's knowledge, Indian Head Spring was always reliable, even in the dry season.

The next source of water, some fifty to sixty miles further, was Tapanic Tank, a grim and lonely place surrounded by tall desert cactus, mesquite shrubs, and rabbit brush. This, too, was quite reliable the year round.

The stretch of desert between Tapanic Tank and the next water was some seventy to eighty miles…and Diago Spring, the last water hole, could not be trusted. It was dry half the time. Scattered bones and human skulls told of men who'd reached the spring and, finding it dry, had laid down and died. Situated in a shallow arroyo, it was encircled by mounds of sand, odd-shaped boulders of varied sizes, mesquite, cactus, and galleta grass. From Diago Spring there was nothing but parched, burning desert all the way to Tucson.

Matt Blake knew that when they rode away from Tapanic Tank, they must be prepared to make their water last on into Tucson. He tried to convince himself that somehow Diago Spring would have water. Even though he knew he was bending the last rule of the desert, the one that says not to count on being lucky, Blake was willing to take the odds. It was worth it to bring a killer like McClain to justice.

The lawman narrowed his deep-blue eyes against the painful glare reflecting from the desert. There was the caste of the desert upon him. He was a tall man, broad in shoulder, narrow in hip. Little rivulets of sweat ran down the deep furrows in his handsome leathered face and lost themselves in his shirt and vest. Along with the silver tips in his temples, side-burns, and moustache, they spelled out all his forty-one years.

The dusty, grey Stetson was dipped low over his brow, giving partial shade to his eyes. His shirt, clean and white at the beginning of the day, was now clinging to his back, caked with a thin film of Arizona dust. His sweat-soaked vest was of black cowhide. On his right hip, he wore a tied-down Colt .45 in a black holster. In his saddle scabbard was a Winchester repeater rifle. He knew how to use them both.

Sharp of eye and steady of nerve, he wielded the Winchester with uncanny accuracy. As for the Colt, men now lay six feet beneath the sod who had challenged the speed and precision of Blake's hand.

Far to the east and south of Blake's chosen path, a band of renegade Apaches had been tracked down to the south of Gila Bend by a platoon of cavalry out of Fort Simms.

The renegades were malcontents who had risen up against Chief Abondi, the revered leader of the Apache nation. According to Samanti, leader of the renegades, there were not enough white men being tortured and killed. Samanti declared he lived only for afflicting and murdering the whites.

In open, verbal conflict with Abondi, the young rebel leader demanded more aggressive attacks on wagon trains, stagecoaches, and travelers in general. Abondi had proven his own ability for violence, but a crazy thirst for blood was beyond him. Samanti and his followers were severed from the Apache nation by the prudent chief.

In the heat of anger, Samanti and his ninety-three followers rode out of the Apache village. They were now free to plot
their own course, to kill and plunder all over southwest
Arizona. As Abondi had foreseen, they soon drew the attention of the U.S. Cavalry.

Lieutenant William Taylor headed up the platoon of forty-
five men after the renegades. Standing just over six feet, Taylor
carried nearly two hundred pounds on his well-proportioned
frame. He looked like he had been in uniform all his life as he
sat tall and erect in the saddle. His eyes, narrow from squinting
into sun and wind, were a cool gray, and said the man was military all the way to the bone.

Riding at his left flank was his platoon sergeant, Jed
Cooley. He was not quite as tall as his senior officer, but he
outweighed him by fifty pounds. The big sergeant had red
hair—and the temper that went with it. Fighting Indians was
his meat. Throughout the West, he had tangled with Utes,
Kiowas, Sioux, Comanches, Cheyennes, Yaquis, and the vio-
lent Apaches.

Cooley was fast on his feet for a big man. He had killed
Indians with his bare hands in hand-to-hand combat. He
could break a man's neck without effort. And as more than
one rebellious soldier had learned, the big redhead could
punch harder than a mule could kick.

"We've got 'em cornered, Lieutenant!" cried Cooley.

Samanti and his band were riding hard toward a giant
crested butte. It was surrounded by gullies and boulders.

"There's only about twenty of them, Sergeant," cried
Taylor. "When they run up against the butte, tell the men to

dismount and take cover!"

One side of the butte was fractured by a crevice with a sheer drop of thirty to forty feet. The cavalry was coming around the other side in a semicircular formation, closing in fast. It was apparent the Indians were in trouble. The butte was too steep for the horses to climb.

"If they dismount and start to climb the butte, we can pick 'em off like rats in a barrel!" Cooley shouted.

As the Apaches approached the butte, the platoon was less than four hundred yards behind. The semi-circle of thundering horses and riders raised a giant cloud of red dust. Lieutenant Taylor unsheathed his saber, lifted it high over his head, and shouted, "Charge!"

The bugler sounded the signal. The cavalrymen were lifting carbines to their shoulders when they saw them. A swarm of whooping Apaches had come over the crest, their mounts sliding down the steep side of the butte.

"It's a trap!" shouted the astonished lieutenant. "Sound the retreat!"

The bugler blasted the retreat signal. Horses went skidding in the dust. Within seconds the platoon had done a full turn. Reining his horse in close to the young officer, Sergeant Cooley shouted, "Most of their horses are fresh. We can't outrun 'em! We're outnumbered two to one!"

"We'll have to make a stand! Head for those gullies off to the right!"

The fresh Indian mounts were gaining on the platoon. Apache rifles began to bark.

"Spread out!" shouted Taylor. "Head for those gullies!"

Few men could hear over the wind in their ears and the thunder of hooves. The lieutenant pointed his saber off to the right. The men caught the signal and veered.

One of the cavalry horses caught a bullet in the flank. As it went down, the soldier rolled in the dirt, dropping his carbine. The charging Apaches were coming straight for him. He drew his pistol, took aim, and fired. One of the lead Indians went down, taking his horse with him as he pitched over its head. Then a bullet caught the soldier in the chest, another in the stomach. He never felt the hooves.

Reaching the first row of arroyos, the soldiers uncinched their saddles, dropping them to the ground. If they lost their horses, they must have their saddles. In the saddlebags each man carried four hundred rounds of ammunition.

The burning sun looked down from the sky as clouds of dust rolled up from the hooves of painted ponies. The renegades charged to within twenty yards of the arroyo fortress and the acrid smell of gunpowder filled the air. Indians and soldiers alike were dropping. Pools of blood ran out onto the sand, bright red for a moment before the desert sucked away the color and left only a patch of dull brown.

The Apaches came in waves, galloping, whooping, shooting, hating… Even if Sheriff Blake had know of the cavalry platoon's plight, he was only one man, and besides, he was too far away to help. But if he had been aware of the renegades' council as they had planned the trap for the pursuing soldiers, he would have been very uneasy. For what was left of a band of renegade Yaqui Indians was making its way south to a rendezvous with Samanti. And, at the moment, they were a few miles south of Blake and his prisoner.

Sharing Samanti's love for bloodshed and the hatred for whites, the Yaquis had left their tribe in Walnut Canyon in the north over a hundred strong. Twice on their way south they had encountered cavalry forces from Fort Prescott and, outnumbered, had been cut to eighteen men. Their original leader, Yellow Fang, had been killed.

They were out of water…and had been for days. Three of their horses had already dropped. When the first one went down, they slit its throat. They drank its blood but the thickened blood had only intensified their thirst.

With swollen tongues and cracked lips, the Yaquis talked of white travelers who camped in the desert at night. If they spotted them before dark, or their campfires after dark, they would be able to kill them and take their water.

Young Gray Wolf had assumed charge of the band. The other seventeen respected him. He had killed more whites than any of the others. His high cheekbones and humped nose blended with the sharp features of his handsome face, and he was broad shouldered and thick of chest. His arms were especially muscular. The biceps bulged, forcing the veins to the surface of the skin. He moved like a cat, smooth and methodical. Astride his pinto, he seemed a part of the animal. But even the powerful Gray Wolf was showing signs of dehydration.

The Yaquis were unfamiliar with the desert territory. Somehow they had assumed there would be frequent water holes. The sun seemed to burn holes into their eyes. Worst of all, four of the men were wounded. Gray Wolf was amazed that any of the four were still alive.

The wounded had to ride. The remaining eleven horses plodded slowly. Each carried a man while three horseless men walked. And the great ball of fire in the cloudless sky seemed to smile in mockery as it drained the moisture from their bodies.

Buzzards flying overhead circled for a while, then flew away. The dust lifting from the desert floor intensified their thirst. Men and horses were slowly losing strength.

"We must find Samanti," Gray Wolf said in his native Yaqui. "They will have food, water, and ammunition."

"Yes," replied Talking Rifle, "when we ride with Samanti, we will have need of nothing. We will live with abundance of everything."

"Gray Wolf!" cried one of the braves on foot. The leader turned toward the voice behind him. One of the wounded men had fallen to the ground.

Gray Wolf dismounted and knelt beside the fallen man. "He is dead," he said.

"So is High Hawk," replied another. "He has been dead for many hours. I have said nothing. Is it not best to bury the dead together?" Somehow High Hawk's body had adhered to his horse's back.

The Yaquis had no tools for burial. Gray Wolf knew that even with tools none of them had the strength to dig two graves. Overhead he heard the screech of the buzzards. The carrion birds had returned.

"Somehow they knew," Gray Wolf said to himself. He raised his eyes toward the yellow sky. Turning to his dusty followers, he said, "We will cover the bodies with rocks."

The crude burial completed, the weary band continued southward. The sun moved slowly. Each step was becoming more of an effort for man and horse.

Gray Wolf ran his tongue over dry lips. He thought of the sparkling springs and babbling brooks in Walnut Canyon. He daydreamed of the giant spruce trees casting their shadows across grassy hills. Somehow in his mind's eye, he could see the snow on Humphrey's Peak, northwest of Walnut Canyon. He thought of the cold winds that cooled the canyon like frosty breath hurled against the jagged walls of granite.

Suddenly he heard the heavy thud. One of the horses had collapsed, spilling its rider. The weary rider slowly got to his feet. The horse never would.

"We cannot spare a bullet," said Gray Wolf, "but the animal must suffer no more." He drew his knife and plunged it into the horse's heart. Then he slit its throat.

"Gray Wolf!" cried Talking Rifle. "Riders! Two of them."

The horse had fallen just as the weary band had topped a casual rise. Gray Wolf jumped up and joined the excited brave who pointed to the south. Two riders were making their way slowly toward the northeast. At times the distant figures seemed to dance as their images filtered through shimmering waves of heat. Gray Wolf smiled at Talking Rifle.

Through squinted eyes, the sheriff scanned the country before him. This was a lonely land, its surface cracked and shattered into shallow arroyos. There were deeper dried basins, their floors covered with broken clusters of lava, long cooled from ages when volcanoes were active. It was a land made to be forgotten by men who loved grassy prairies or productive farmland.

Now and then a little desert creature would scurry across their path. Long-tailed lizards sunned themselves on blistered boulders. Occasionally a buzzard would take flight from some distant rock, lifting itself toward the sky seemingly without effort.

The blazing sun sauntered in its afternoon descent. Checking it as infrequently as you could bear, it still seemed at a standstill. The horses' hooves raised little clouds of dust with each muffled step. The only other sound in the two riders' ears was the uneven squeaking of the two saddles.

Matt Blake wiped the stinging sweat from his eyes with the sleeve of his shirt. He had the strange sensation that unseen eyes were watching them. Maybe just the heat. Or Indians? They had a mysterious way of blending in with the desert. A man could be looking right at them and never know it.

Blake tried to wet his parched lips with his tongue. It didn't work. His mouth was dry and dusty. The horses would soon need water. As the two riders approached a group of tall rocks, he saw a large spot of cool shade. Cool, at least in comparison with the open fire of the merciless sun.

"Let's haul up and give the horses a rest," Blake said. Dismounting, he poured a small amount of water from a canteen into his Stetson. He gave it to McClain's horse. The sound of its drinking increased the dryness of his own mouth. A few drops of water fell from the horse's muzzle. As he looked down, the thirsty desert swallowed them instantly. He repeated the operation for his own horse and for the roan pack horse.

"Seems stupid to me," McClain said.

"What's that?"

"Watering the animals first."

"We need these horses, McClain. Without a horse in this desert, a man is dead. Your ration and mine will be five swallows."

McClain cursed violently.

"You give those dumb beasts more than us?"

Ignoring the question, Blake handed up the canteen to McClain, who was still in the saddle.

"Five swallows," the sheriff said.

McClain's foot shot out of the stirrup and kicked the canteen from Blake's hand. The tall man bent over and snatched up the gurgling canteen. As he straightened up, a spurred boot whistled past his ear. Anger shot through him like a bolt of lightening. He gripped McClain's leg and yanked him to the ground with one hand. While the little man rolled in the dirt, he capped the canteen and hung it back on the saddle.

With the speed of a cat, Blake then leaped on the sprawling outlaw. Sinking his hands into McClain's shirt and vest, he picked him up and slammed him against the rock wall that towered over them. The breath gushed from the little man's mouth.

"You and I," the sheriff said, "are going to Tucson. There's a hungry noose waiting for a little beady-eyed killer. I'm going to see that it's fed!"

"As a very famous lawman once said," retorted McClain, breathing heavily, "'We'll see.'"

"Get back in the saddle, we're moving out."

"I want my water ration!" screamed McClain.

"Unless you can squeeze it out of the dust, you don't get any. You just donated your ration to the desert. Mine, too. Saddle up."

Sheriff Matt Blake was usually as accurate with his words as with his gun. McClain was indeed a little beady-eyed killer. Small in stature, he stood barely five feet nine inches tall. He was wiry and slim. His Adam's apple protruded sharply, to match his thin, hooked nose, and his eyes were set close together. Their pale green hue gave him a shifty, mean look. They were cold and hard…the kind of eyes that could send chills down a decent man's spine.

What Duke McClain lacked in size and stature, he made up for in speed with his gun hand. Men who had watched him draw swore that he moved like a machine. Most of the men he had shot down died with their guns still in their holsters. This included those who were facing him—and those he shot in the back. Then, of course, there were the many unarmed men, women, and children he had murdered in cold blood.

The ruthless trio of Rob Chamberlain, Will Nichols, and Hank Ripley had approached McClain after they watched him outdraw and kill two men at once in a Wichita Saloon.

"We can use a fast gun," Chamberlain told McClain over a glass of whiskey. "The boys and me are headin' west. Banks are loadin' up with money. We aim to get our share."

Chamberlain was an ugly man. His nose was flat; his eyes were set wide apart. There were big gaps between what teeth he had. He was better looking, if that were possible, only when he kept his mouth shut. Past thirty, and the eldest of the three, he was the trio's spokesman.

McClain turned the empty glass in his hand, then looked Chamberlain straight in the eye for a long moment. Shifting his stare to Ripley, he poured another shot in the glass.

Ripley was tall and lanky. His features were sharp and pointed with a chin longer than normal. He spoke with a slight stutter. His skin was very white, matching the colorless hair which protruded from under his hat and dangled over his acne-splotched face.

Downing the shot in one swallow, McClain transferred his attention to the last member of the trio, Nichols. He was nearly six feet in height, built with a bull-like neck, and broad, muscular shoulders. His scraggly beard made him look older than his twenty-six years.

"We'll split everything four ways," Chamberlain was saying.

McClain eyed him coldly. "Why don't you three go at it like you have been? Cut it three ways, you'll make more money."

"B-but w-we ain't n-nowhere n-near as fast with a g-gun

as you," Hank Ripley interjected.

"That's right, McClain," added Will Nichols, "we're gonna face a lot of guns. I shore would be willin' to take a smaller cut to have you in the pack!"

"That's how you look at it, too, Chamberlain?" McClain asked, playing with his empty glass.

"Sure is!" replied Chamberlain.

"All right," Duke McClain answered with a firm tone, "I get half and you boys split the other half."

Chamberlain had started to object when he saw that McClain's pale green eyes were now staring into his soul. A cold chill danced on his backbone. For a moment, the three outlaws looked at each other.

McClain pushed his chair back.

"Wait!" Chamberlain said. "It's a deal."

McClain scooted back up to the table. "Let's get one other thing straight," he said with clenched teeth, "I ain't wearin' no mask. We just don't leave no witnesses."

Thus began a reign of terror. Joining up with the three other outlaws in Wichita, McClain would leave a trail of blood across Kansas, Colorado, and New Mexico. Wichita's four banks were held up. All the employees were shot down. Bank customers and people on the streets were murdered as the outlaws blasted their way out of town.

The bloodthirsty quartet made their way across Kansas into Colorado. McClain did most of the killing. Holding a rancher and his family prisoners for several weeks, the outlaws had holed up until things cooled off. Leaving the family dead, they made their way to the town of Burlington, east of Denver.

Coming out of the Burlington bank with guns blazing, they jumped to their saddles and turned their horses to gallop out of town. Spotting a young rancher and his wife blocking their escape in a buckboard, McClain sighted on the man and fired. As the tall, slender man fell backward into the bed of the buckboard, he squeezed off another shot and hit the woman.

The buckboard horses reared and the rawboned rancher came up on his knees, rifle in hand, and blew Ripley from the saddle. McClain spun his horse around. For a split second, the rancher and the outlaw looked each other straight on. The rancher levered another bullet into the chamber. Before he could fire, McClain shot him again. As the man dropped in the buckboard, the outlaw galloped away to catch up with Chamberlain and Nichols.

"Was Ripley dead?" shouted McClain above the thunder of the hooves.

"Think so," Chamberlain shouted back. "He didn't move a muscle when he hit the ground!"

As the outlaws turned their horses toward Denver, Burlington's sheriff and citizens tended to Ripley and rancher William Spain. They were both still alive. Mrs. Spain had died instantly.

Lying on the doctor's table in Burlington, the dying outlaw identified his three comrades. He made sure the sheriff understood that McClain did most of the killing.

William Spain was on the doctor's couch in the same room as the outlaw coughed out his last breath. He heard Ripley's description of McClain. Spain closed his eyes. He could see McClain's ugly face in his mind. The vicious grin exposing yellow teeth. The matching yellow hair protruding from under his hat. The same repugnant picture tortured his brain again when weeks later he stood over Mary Anne's grave.

"I'll get him, my darling," he said, his tears falling to the mound of dirt. "I'll get him, if it's the last thing I do!"

The "wanted" posters dispatched from the U.S. Marshal's office in Denver tagged him as Duke "Mad-dog" McClain. Sheriff Matt Blake's first knowledge of him came the day those posters arrived in Tucson. The dispatch noted Ripley's death and indicated that the remaining three outlaws had split up. McClain had single-handedly shot and killed several people in southern Colorado after the trio had held up two Denver banks.

Rob Chamberlain and Will Nichols went on to hold up a bank in Gunnison and another in Blanding, Utah. McClain was next seen in New Mexico. He seemed to be heading toward Tucson. The "Mad-dog" had left a wake of ranchers and their families savagely murdered between Santa Fe and Silver City.

McClain did come to Tucson, one night after dark and two days ahead of the "wanted" posters. He went into a saloon for a drink and his fancy fell on one of the dance-hall girls. She rejected his advances, turning her attention to another man. McClain called her a whore. She stung his face with a well-aimed slap. Enraged, he shot her down in front of a crowd of witnesses. In the midst of blazing guns, he got away into the night.

Matt Blake formed a posse and went after him. In the vastness of the desert, McClain eluded them. Dejected, the posse returned to Tucson. When the sheriff discovered who McClain was from the poster, he had gritted his teeth and said, "This is one lowdown snake that has got to be stopped!" The telegraph office was closed, but its clerk knew better than to argue when the sheriff dragged him out of bed to send some urgent messages.

For nothing, it soon seemed. Several weeks passed and the little killer had apparently disappeared. Blake figured that maybe the Apaches had killed him. Then came the telegraph message from the sheriff in Yuma.

```
MAD-DOG MCCLAIN IN YUMA STOP
KNOW YOU WANT HIM FOR MURDER IN TUCSON
STOP TAKE NEXT STAGE TO YUMA STOP
    WILL HANKINS, SHERIFF
```

Two days later, Sheriff Matt Blake sat in Sheriff Will Hankins' office discussing Hankins' plan as easily as if he were hunting deer and not an unpredictable killer. McClain was still in Yuma all right, staying at the Arizona Hotel. Every night after eating in the hotel restaurant, the pint-sized outlaw headed for the Silver Spur Saloon. Seated alone at a table with his back to the wall, he spent each evening polishing off a bottle of whiskey. He kept a watchful eye on the door.

Gambling that McClain would follow his newly established pattern, the two lawmen set the trap. By arrangement with the owner of the Silver Spur, ten deputized men would be seated at tables and standing at the bar. At a given signal, all ten men would level their six-guns on McClain.

This little outlaw did not disappoint them. He took his usual position. When everything seemed just right, the barkeep was to drop a whiskey bottle on the floor in front of the bar.

It came off without a hitch. When the bottle crashed to the floor, McClain checked out the noise. He looked down at the spilling whiskey and the shattered glass. When he looked up, eleven barrels were aimed at his slender body. One was that of Sheriff Matt Blake.

"You're under arrest for murder," Blake said. "You're going to Tucson with me to stand trial."

McClain gave up without a struggle.

At dawn the next day, Sheriff Hankins opened the cell door. Matt Blake stepped into the cell.

"Put your wrists together."

The outlaw looked at him with those cold, narrow-set eyes. Slowly, he moved one wrist over the other.

"You may put a rope on my wrists, Blake, but you'll never put one on my neck." Matt Blake cinched the knot with a jerk. McClain clenched his teeth.

"I promise you—you'll never get me to Tucson."

"We'll see," said Blake.

Those words came back again to Blake as he scanned the desert trail still ahead of them. The afternoon sun was sliding down the western sky. Soon there would be relief from the cruel heat. The desert's emptiness lay all about them, still and monotonous. The few marks men could make on this vast expanse were usually swept away by the night winds. There was life here—insects, birds, and snakes—though nothing stirred at the moment. Quietly, men and horses moved on.

McClain noticed that the sheriff was bending over in the saddle, studying the ground. "A pair of wagons seem to be headed in the same direction we are," he said to McClain. "I'd say they're about half a day ahead of us." The outlaw made no comment. Nothing more was said for over an hour.

"Why didn't we take the stage to Tucson?" McClain muttered, breaking the silence.

"I didn't want to put any driver, guard, or passengers in a position of danger."

"Danger? Are you afraid of me, tall man?"

"Nope. Just cautious."

"Why are we making' our own trail? Why don't we follow the road of the stagecoach?"

Blake looked at McClain through squinted eyes and said, "Too many of your kind riding the stagecoach trails. Might meet up with some who would see the rope on your wrists and the star on my shirt. Besides, it's shorter this way."

"I told you, Sheriff," McClain said with a sly smile, "lot of things can happen 'tween here and Tucson."

The western sky was now a cluster of orange and red as the last flames of the sun slipped over the horizon. A breeze began to cool the sweating horses and dust-caked riders.

"Got about half an hour of light left. We can just make that bunch of tall rocks up ahead. By early tomorrow afternoon we should be to Indian Head Spring. There'll be water there."

McClain shrugged in reply.

The rock cluster proved to be centered on a shallow arroyo. The slender rocks lifting their heads fifty, maybe sixty feet into the air dwarfed the giant saguaros. The arroyo itself ran along between smooth rock walls averaging eight to ten feet in height. Mesquite was scattered all over the area.

The floor of the arroyo was covered with a generous depth of soft sand. It would make a good place to bed down for the night.

Pulling the dun to a halt in the arroyo, Sheriff Matt Blake dismounted. He glanced up at McClain who was smiling broadly. The little outlaw's yellow stringy hair was hanging over his collar and sticking out from under his black flat-crowned hat. And the teeth in that smile were the same color as his hair.

"What are you smiling about?"

"I was just thinking. It's still a long way to Tucson. You will never put a noose on me, Sheriff."

"We'll see," said Blake.

"Can I have some water now?"

Blake set his jaw. "After the horses get theirs."

Lifting the Stetson from his head, Blake slapped it against his leg. The dust flew off in puffs. He watered the horses and then gave McClain his share. As he tilted the canteen upward for his own portion, he again felt the unseen eyes.

CHAPTER TWO

With shaded fingers, darkness came to the desert. While the tall sheriff unsaddled and tethered the horses, the little outlaw walked around the rock-encircled gully. Stepping out beyond the rocks, he stood facing westward and watched the dying light on the horizon. Fumbling with a tobacco pouch, he rolled himself a cigarette.

McClain stood there for some time after the last glimmer of light had faded away, thinking.

Returning to Blake, he saw that a fire was crackling, lighting up the arroyo and casting menacing shadows on the rock walls.

The man from Tucson was brushing and currying the horses.

"Untie my hands, Sheriff," he said with a friendly tone, "and I'll help you with that."

"'S all right. I'll handle it," Blake answered in a level monotone.

"My wrists are getting rope burn."

"Your neck is going to have it, too."

A deep frown came over the outlaw's face. "You don't like me, do you, Blake?"

Blake popped the currycomb against the brush, walked over to where his saddle lay on the ground, and knelt down. Unbuckling the straps on his saddlebag, he returned the comb and brush to their place, just on top of McClain's revolver. "Nope, I don't like you," he answered. "I don't like what you did to Margie Kendall."

"Wouldn't have happened if she'd treated me decent."

"So she didn't cotton to you. Was that reason to gun her down?"

"She had it coming! She sure wasn't cold-shouldering them other men."

Matt Blake was pouring water from a canteen into a well-worn coffee pot. "What about all the others you killed?" he asked.

"The only other's I killed was in fair gunfights," McClain said. "I'm fast, mister…mighty fast!"

"Yeah, you're so fast some of them didn't even have a chance to turn around before you shot 'em in the back."

Fury filled the outlaw's face. With his breath whistling through his teeth, he reached down and grabbed a burning mesquite branch from the fire. He lunged at Blake, who was kneeling beside the fire, and swung the blazing mass toward his head.

The experienced lawman rolled away. By the time McClain had leaped over the fire to begin another swing, Blake was on his feet. Off balance from the second attempt, the outlaw spun around to meet a right cross. The blow snapped his head back, flattened him on his back. More stars were visible than those in the Arizona sky.

He felt himself being lifted into space. Suddenly he was slammed to his rump. Shaking his head, McClain tried desperately to clear his vision. As his eyes focused again, he stared over the fire at the tall man, who had returned to his mess duties.

Wiping blood from his mouth on his sleeve, Duke McClain said, "You don't really think I'm going to swing from that rope, do you, mister tall man?"

"If you don't hang, it'll be because you tried something asinine and I had to kill you."

"You wouldn't be so tough if my hands weren't tied. It'd be a different story, then, mister!"

"Shut your mouth, sonny. I was eating little boys like you for breakfast before I was half your age."

"Big man," McClain said with a sneer as he spit a stream of blood into the fire. "You wouldn't face me in a standoff gunfight."

"That would be a real temptation. But my desire to see you swing from a rope is stronger. Straight out killing you would be too good for you. I want you to think about that noose for a while. I want you to lie awake all night in a cold sweat, dreading the dawning of the day of your hanging."

McClain daubed his sleeve repeatedly on his swollen lip. His eyes blinked and fluttered, as Blake continued.

"I want you to feel your knees weaken as you approach the gallows. I want you to see the face of every man, woman, and child that you murdered in cold blood, glaring at you from the shadows. I want you..."

"Mad-dog" McClain scrambled in the sand and jumped

to his feet. "Shut up! Shut up! The only person I murdered was that saloon female! Nobody else, d'ya hear me? Nobody!"

Blake, standing up, pushed his hat back on his head. "What about those poor men and women on those stage-coaches?"

"That wasn't me! I never done it!"

"And what about those innocent ranchers? What about their wives and children?"

Blake's shadow, thrown against the tall rocks by the fire, made him seem like a menacing giant. McClain was shaking his head. "No! No! It wasn't me!"

The sheriff appeared to swell in size. McClain's fear was mingled with wrath. The wrath was surfacing. The hollow voice of his accuser was saying, "What about those bank employees?"

The rage overtook him and he shouted, "They had it com—" His eyes were bulging. He swallowed hard.

Blake stared him down for what seemed an endless time. The dancing shadows on the rock walls seemed to mock "Mad-dog" McClain.

"Yeah, I know," Blake's voice broke the silence, "like Margie Kendall, they had it coming. For the same kind of twisted, insensible reason."

The spirit had gone out of the young outlaw. He dropped to the sand and sat staring into the fire while Sheriff Blake finished preparing the meal. Not a word passed between them while they devoured their meal of beans, hardtack bread, and coffee.

The night wind began to ruffle the flames of the fire. The

lawman wiped off the tin plates and scoured out the cups with sand, conserving the precious water.

While Blake returned the utensils to their proper places in the saddle gear, McClain stared pensively into the flames. He paid no attention to Blake, who labored near the saddlebags for some time.

After a while, Blake returned and threw some more mesquite branches on the nearly extinguished fire. As the wood began to snap and the flames cracked, McClain looked up at the sheriff.

"Mr. Blake," he said, hardly parting his lips, "I've got a proposition for you."

Blake let a long moment pass. "I'm probably not interested, but let's hear it."

"You know those two banks I held up?"

"Yeah?"

"I've got the money stashed…"

"If you're about to offer a bribe, forget it."

"I don't think you would exactly call this a bribe. As I was sayin'… I've got over ninety thousand stashed away. Nobody but me knows where it is. If I hang, the secret dies with me."

Blake eyed him coldly. "What are you getting at?"

"You're pretty fast with a gun, right?"

"You might say that."

"I've heard that when a man draws on you, he's got a bullet through his heart before he sees the gun in your hand."

Blake shifted his position. "Don't know. None of them that ever drew a gun on me and took a bullet through the heart are around to tell it."

McClain set his cold, beady eyes straight into Blake's. "I think I can beat you."

"Yep."

"Then here's my deal. I'll write down the location of that bank money and put it in my shirt pocket. You let me have my gun. We'll face off square. If you beat me, you can take the note off my corpse. If you don't…"

Blake clenched his teeth. "Like I said…killing you outright is too good for you. I want you to count off the stairs as you climb the gallows. There's a killer's noose waiting for you, 'Mad-dog.' I want you to see it swaying in the wind just before I drop the hood over your face. I want you to feel it cinched around your throat. I hope you hear the screams of those helpless women and children you murdered, as you feel the trap door go under your feet. I hope the drop seems like an eon before your neck snaps!"

McClain snarled like a dog at the words of Matt Blake as they died away in the night. "Don't say I didn't give you your chance, tall man. It's still a long way to Tucson. Sooner or later, I'll get the drop on you."

"It's getting late," Blake said, "we better get some shut-eye. Gonna be another hot one tomorrow." Against much protest, the lawman looped a rope around McClain's lean waist and through his tied wrists. Drawing it tight, he knotted the rope in the small of the back.

"You can't do much with your hands in this position, 'Mad-dog.' Now I'm taking off your boots. Don't think you want to run too far in this desert. Besides…there might be Indians out there."

"Indians?"

"Possible. I've had a feeling about it since midafternoon."

"You mean you let us holler and carry on like we been doin', all the time knowin' there's Indians out there?"

Blake drew his Colt .45, spun the cylinder, and checked the load. Holstering it, he unsheathed the Winchester from the scabbard and checked it out. "Wouldn't have made any difference. If they're out there, they saw us. They didn't need to hear us. Anyway, they don't travel at night."

McClain lay down on his side, placing his head on his saddle. "Sheriff, would you mind layin' my blanket over me? I can't do it with my hands tied down like this."

Blake responded to the outlaw's request. McClain, muttering to himself, said, "Sure is mighty uncomfortable." He swore at the rope, then at the sheriff.

"S'pose you think those people you made lie down on the floors of those stagecoaches while you shot them to death were comfortable," said Blake.

McClain had no more to say. The tall man sat down on the sand and removed his boots. The night air felt cool on his feet.

As the fire dwindled to dying embers, the outlaw fell asleep. Blake noted his even, steady breathing. The desert-wise lawman knew he must sleep lightly. The feeling that the two weary riders were not alone crept over him again.

Pulling the blanket up around his eyes, he wondered how the desert could be a furnace in the day and an iceberg at night. The night wind played a mournful tune on the rocks. Blake's sensitive ears caught the rustle of small creatures moving about.

Listening intently, he assured himself that the noises were just small creatures.

Weary as he was, sleep seemed to evade him. His every bone seemed to complain that it had been taxed to the limit. He cupped his hands behind his head. Looking upward, he was suddenly aware of the great winkling canopy overhead. There was no moon, but it seemed that God had hung out every one of His stars for display that night. Matt Blake felt very small and insignificant. "What a little speck of nothingness I am," he thought to himself.

He dropped his right hand to the Winchester. Straining his ears for any abnormal sound, he listened to the night. The horses were quiet. McClain was sleeping soundly. Pulling his Stetson down over his face, he tried to relax. The feeling of unwanted company crawled over him again. Was it just his imagination? He still felt wide awake.

Lying there with his head on the saddle and his hat pulled low, his thoughts drifted back to Jeannie. How wonderful were those two years of marriage. Jeannie had married him, knowing that he was born to be a lawman. That six-gun was as much a part of him as his right hand itself. She never asked him to change. She loved him. His way of life would be hers.

What a beautiful day it was when she had scurried down the dusty street from Doc Sanders' place to the sheriff's office.

"It's confirmed," she said with a lilt in her voice. "The baby will be born in September!" He remembered how he picked her up and whirled her around the office. Holding her in his arms, he kissed her and said, "Mrs. Blake, you have made me the happiest man alive! We'll call him Adam David

Blake after his two grandfathers."

"Him, is it? And what if it's a girl?"

"Why, darling, Blakes always have boys first!"

Her gay laughter echoed off the walls. He could almost hear it again…but no, it was only the desert wind wrapping itself around the rock wall of the arroyo.

With that familiar touch of sadness, he remembered again the darkest day of his life.

"I'm sorry, Matt," Doc Sanders' voice trembled, "I couldn't save her."

"What about the baby?" Blake could hear himself saying.

"Baby was dead before she was, Matt. It was a boy."

Twelve long, lonely years had passed, but the memories still played hard on the strings of his heart. His thoughts of Jeannie soon gave way to sleep as the night winds scurried across the desert sands.

The two riders slowly making their way northeastward were no doubt well supplied with water. Thirsty, but cautious, Gray Wolf and his men had kept a safe distance between themselves and the two riders. "We will wait for our chance," Gray Wolf said to Talking Rifle. "They will make camp at sunset. We will have their water by sunrise tomorrow morning."

The little band of Yaqui Indians silently prayed to their gods to somehow relieve the intense heat. It was to no avail. Even the anticipation of water by morning did not give them renewed strength. They could only think of their present agony.

Gray Wolf heard the soft thump of one of the men falling to the earth. Kneeling in a circle around the fallen man, they watched him die. "We must gather more rocks for burial," Gray Wolf said.

Scanning the area, Gray Wolf was quickly aware that there were few rocks available. "We will take him further until we find more rocks."

Four men struggled, lifting the dead man's body onto one of the horses. The thirsty men and horses plodded on. "We have lost sight of the riders," Talking Rifle said to Gray Wolf.

"We must find them again," the muscular Indian replied. "Take two men on horses and go on ahead. We must keep them in sight."

The three Indian horses obeyed their riders, but showed rebellion at being pushed to hurry across the burning desert. The group left behind watched them go through a cloud of dust.

Suddenly another brave fell to the ground. His tongue had swollen. He wallowed in the dust, choking. His eyes were wild. He died, clawing at this throat.

The inferno in the sky and the parched earth had joined to squeeze the life from them…one at a time.

While they were lifting the second dead man to another horse's back, another brave stumbled to the ground. Delirious, he rolled and twisted in the dust. His eyes rolled back. Muttering in a soft voice, he spoke of streams of water, then stopped breathing.

Despair was gripping the entire band. Watching their blood brothers dying in such agony was stirring panic.

"Gray Wolf!" cried one of the braves. "You must do something!"

"Where is your beloved Samanti?" one cried.

"All of this is your fault!" cried another.

"We should have turned back when Yellow Fang was killed," another was saying, "but you told us Samanti was your friend. He would take us in and we would live in abundance. Look at us!"

The thirst-crazed brave was half out of his mind. He jerked the knife from his waistband and lunged at Gray Wolf. The young, muscular leader dodged the whistling blade. Lifting himself from the dust, the crazed brave came hard at Gray Wolf again. A powerful fist pummeled him to the ground.

"Do not do this thing!" Gray Wolf shouted. "Do not make me harm you!"

The wild man leaped to his feet. With a savage scream, he came again, aiming the knife at Gray Wolf's heart. The agile leader sidestepped, grasped the knife-hand. Twisting it inward, he thrust the knife into the crazed man's belly.

They both stood there as if frozen. Gray Wolf felt the warm, smooth liquid flowing on his hand. The mortally wounded man's forehead came to rest on Gray Wolf's chest, then he tilted his head back and looked into Gray Wolf's face. The wildness had gone out of his eyes. "Gray Wolf," he gasped, "I am sorry." His eyes closed. Blood was running from his mouth. The muscular leader eased the dead man to the ground.

Tears found their way to Gray Wolf's eyes. "My brother,"

he said with a broken voice, "why did you make me do it?"

The incident had its effect. The moment of panic was over.

"Put him on my horse," Gray Wolf said. "We will bury him with the others."

One of the braves pointed to the southeast. A Yaqui buck was trotting back toward them on a sweaty pinto.

"We find riders," he said on approach. "They stop to rest in shade of tall rocks. Have much water."

Almost to a man, the Indians licked their lips at the sound of the word. "We will move on now," said Gray Wolf. Slowly the ten men and twelve horses turned their faces to the southeast. Only the dead men rode. The others walked.

The afternoon sun dropped slowly down from the western sky. "Soon there will be relief from the heat," Gray Wolf said.

As the sun dipped into the western horizon in a cluster of orange and red flame, the group caught up to Talking Rifle's companion. "Talking Rifle up ahead," he said, pointing. "He keep riders in sight."

As darkness enveloped the desert in a cool shroud, the little band of Yaquis was piling rocks on their dead. Gray Wolf and Talking Rifle knelt on the butte overlooking the long slope to the south. "The riders will camp among those rocks." Talking Rifle said, pointing. The rocks were barely visible in the gathering darkness.

"We must plan carefully," Gray Wolf said. "These men have food and water. We are weak. They are strong."

"There is trouble between them," said Talking Rifle.

"They fight at tall rocks. One man very tall. Other man very short. Tall man throw short man against rock, very hard."

"We have little ammunition," Gray Wolf said. "We must surprise them and kill them quickly."

"Maybe best we kill them with knives," suggested Talking Rifle. "Could be army patrol from Fort Simms somewhere near. Sound of guns would bring them. We are in no condition to fight army."

"You are right," agreed Gray Wolf. "We must kill them with knives. We will attack at dawn."

As did most red men, the Yaquis avoided conflict with enemies at night. In their primitive religion, they believed that to die at night would render their spirit forever homeless. The lost spirit would wander endlessly with no happy hunting ground. Gray Wolf and his men would attack at dawn.

"I will take three men," Talking Rifle suggested to Gray Wolf. "We will approach rocks just before light come in east. I will leave men short distance away and crawl to look upon riders. When all looks right, I will give bird signal. All four of us will attack and kill them."

Gray Wolf understood Talking Rifle's intentions. The leader should not risk his life. The others needed him to lead them to Samanti.

"Take the strongest men," said Gray Wolf. "Each one will take his rifle, but only use it if necessary."

Each brave had a single shot Spencer .56. That is, all except Talking Rifle. He had taken a new Winchester .44 repeater from a wagon train which they had plundered several months earlier. He had had another name from birth, but when he acquired the Winchester which could rapidly fire off seven rounds, he found his new name.

"Be careful with your rifle," warned Gray Wolf. "If you should stumble in the darkness, it could go off."

"Do not worry, my brother," replied Talking Rifle, "I will make sure that does not happen."

Looking toward the rock-encircled arroyo where Blake and McClain were camped, the Yaquis could see the light of a small fire. For several moments they could hear the high-pitched voice of one man shouting. Then all was quiet.

The Indians had a few small sacks of corn meal. Passing them around as they sat cross-legged in a circle, they tried to eat. It was to no avail. Their mouths were too dry. Even the horses shook their heads. They could not swallow either.

"We will have water by morning," Gray Wolf said. "Let us rest now."

Lying flat on the ground, the dozen red men from Walnut Canyon tried to sleep. Gray Wolf lay on his back, looking up at the stars. His mind was pondering the events of the day. He thought of the men they had buried under the rocks. He thought of the hungry buzzards in their endless search for meat.

He felt the dried blood on his hand. There had been no way to wash it off. Somewhere within the cry of the night wind, Gray Wolf could hear the voice of the brave whose blood was on his hand. "We should have turned back when Yellow Fang was killed but you told us Samanti was your friend. He would take us in and we would live in abundance. Look at us!"

"Where is your beloved Samanti?" he heard another dying brave say.

"Poor thirst-crazed fools," he thought, "have they forgotten that Samanti is to meet us at the big rock that is shaped like an Indian's head?" According to directions given by Samanti's messenger, the meeting place was at least another day's ride.

He thought of how Samanti, as he gathered troops to fight the white men, had sent a messenger into northern Arizona to confer with Yellow Fang. Samanti desired Yellow Fang to gather up the renegades among the Yaquis and join him within two weeks at Indian Head Spring. Together they would form a small army and live well off the whites.

He remembered how Samanti's messenger had asked to see Gray Wolf. A special message to Gray Wolf from Samanti: "Come and join me, my old friend. We will ride the wind together and make the whites suffer for what they have done to the Indian!"

Agreement was made by Yellow Fang. Whichever band reached Indian Head Spring first would send up smoke signals daily until the other band arrived. The smoke signals would alert the late ones that their friends were there waiting.

"Come and join me, my old friend."

"Your beloved Samanti."

"You told us Samanti was your friend."

These words seemed to reverberate through the chambers of his mind. His thoughts drifted back over the years. He remembered the day he met Samanti. The Apaches and the Yaquis were having a powwow. It lasted over a week. The children played together. Gray Wolf and Samanti, being the same age, became steady playmates. By the time the powwow was over, the two little boys had become fast friends.

Gray Wolf smiled to himself, lying there on the desert floor, as he remembered the day Samanti left. He had stood under a giant spruce tree on the edge of Walnut Canyon, waving goodbye while hot tears scalded his cheeks.

Then he thought of their next meeting, when again the two nations held a powwow. The boys were then both fourteen. For ten days they hunted together, running through the forest of Walnut Canyon. He smiled again as he thought of their wrestling together in the tall grass. Samanti was not as strong as Gray Wolf, but because of his love for the young Apache, sometimes he let Samanti win. Samanti never knew his victories were not real.

While the cool desert wind tingled his dusty face with a thousand little fingers, Gray Wolf let his mind drift to their last meeting. His teeth clenched with the bitter memory.

The whites had come to Arizona Territory with hundreds of cavalrymen. Forts were built at strategic spots. Years before, the whites had made treaties with the tribes in the territory, promising the Indians they could keep their hunting grounds.

The white men had proved to be liars. Now they were going against their promises. They were taking away the Indians' land. The Apaches, in retaliation, had gone on the warpath. Their Yaqui allies had joined them.

U.S. Army troops were brought in to stop the Indian uprising. They would first separate the two tribes. The Apaches must go to the burning desert in the south. The smaller Yaqui nation would remain in the north. The forts were built and manned to enforce the white man's law.

On a cold, wintry day, just outside of Flagstaff, the army general met with the chief of the Apaches and the chief of the Yaquis. The Indian braves and their families waited in the bitter cold.

Gray Wolf and Samanti, now twenty years of age, renewed their friendship. They talked together of old times. Eventually their conversation turned to revenge against the white man.

Samanti was concerned that his chief was showing signs of weakness. Abondi was tired of fighting. The white man had better weapons and equipment. Samanti had been talking to Yellow Fang, a Yaqui brave who was in his thirties and battlewise. The two agreed that the white man must be punished for his lies.

Gray Wolf found himself in full accord with his friend. As they parted, they shook hands Indian style and agreed. "Someday," said Samanti, "we will have revenge on the white man together!"

That was five years ago. Now they were going to be together again. They would fill their cup of vengeance with the blood of the lying white man: Gray Wolf's heart quickened as he though of killing the men who had taken their land and taken the lives of so many of their blood brothers.

His eyelids grew heavy and soon he slept, accepting the gift of rest offered by the cool night wind.

Hours had passed when he was awakened by movement about him. Talking Rifle was giving last minute instructions to his three companions. The other Indians were stirring and lifting their heads. Gray Wolf stood up sleepily. Straining his eyes against the darkness, he went over to Talking Rifle.

"Are you ready to go?" he whispered.

"Yes. Each man will take his place a hundred paces from the gully. One to the east, one to the west, one to the south. I will go from the north. At my signal, they will come quickly. We will attack from all directions at once."

Gray Wolf turned his eyes toward the east. "Go quickly," he said. "It will be dawn soon."

Matt Blake had been asleep for quite some time. As he rolled on his back he found himself suddenly wide awake. Something had disturbed his slumber. What was it? The outlaw was lying motionless, his breathing a monotonous whisper.

The Tucson sheriff strained his ears. The wind was lighter now. Dawn was approaching. It was that darkest few minutes just before light would break on the eastern horizon.

Something had awakened him. Was it an abnormal sound or just a disturbance of his sixth sense? One of the horses snorted.

Blake rolled to his knees, Winchester in hand. Making sure the Colt was in his tied-down holster, he slowly made his way to the horses. They were noticeably nervous. He rubbed each horse's nose, calming them.

In his stocking feet, the tall man made his way to the rock wall on the north side of the gully. A strange silence hovered in the air. The horses were satisfied, once aware of Blake's movement. Outside of the soft, pre-dawn breeze, the only sound was the steady breathing of the sleeping outlaw.

Crouching low against the base of the rock wall, Matt Blake waited. It would be dawn soon. If there were Indians out there, they would attack at the first glimmer of the sun's light.

Suddenly, right above him, he could hear the soft breathing of another man. Flattening his back against the wall, he tilted his head upward. The sky had begun to show a hint of light. He could see the Indian's head, silhouetted against the sky. The top of his rifle barrel protruded over the ledge.

Indian fighting was not new to Matt Blake. He was wise and experienced at the task. One Indian would precede the others as a scout. When the situation was just right, a pre-arranged signal as if part of the natural noises would be given, and the others would attack.

The lawman knew he must kill the Indian silently. He thought of the hunting knife in his saddlebag. But it was forty feet away. It was already a miracle that the red man had not seen him.

There was another way. He would have to kill the Indian with his bare hands. Ever so easy, he eased the Winchester down flat on the sand. He eyed the distance between himself and the Indian. The wall was about eight feet high. By standing up straight, he could grasp the Indian and pull him down.

His first task would be to keep the red man from crying out. Then he must complete the kill. In spite of the cool breeze, Blake's face was beady with sweat. He ran his sleeve over his eyes. The way his heart was pounding reminded him of a blacksmith's hammer. The Indian started to move.

With the swiftness of a cougar, the agile sheriff lunged

upward, sinking his steel grip into the Indian's flesh and then slamming him down into the sand. The brave's rifle flew over Blake's head and hit the ground with a muffled thud. As the red man rolled over, Blake chopped his Adam's apple with the edge of his open hand.

Choking and gasping for breath, the Indian came to his feet, pulling a knife. A rawboned fist whistled through the air. With a sickening crunch, the red man went down. Blake heard the knife hit the sand.

The Indian was shaking his head, trying to find his feet again. Blake looked around for the knife. Dawn was sifting a gray light from the east, but not enough. Where was that knife?

Still choking, the savage lunged at the sheriff's tall form. Matt Blake met him halfway with a crunching blow to the jaw. He staggered and fell, face downward. Blake again looked for the knife. Gone! It must have sunk into the sand.

The Indian gasped and choked. He was trying to get up on his knees. Blake sprang on his back, pushing his face into the soft sand. The red man struggled, but Blake's weight and strength overpowered him. Gasping for breath, he sucked in dust from the desert sand, and coughed. With arms like spring steel, Blake pushed his face into the sand. The Indian's body jumped in spasms for several moments. Gritting his teeth, the lawman held the brave's face hard in the sand.

When all movement ceased, Blake let go of the Indian's head with his left hand and felt the side of the neck for a pulse. There was none.

Still on his knees, Blake heard a sound behind him. He spun around. By the dawn's light, he saw McClain. He was lying on his back and had the dead Indian's rifle aimed right between Blake's eyes. The outlaw's wrists were twisted hard against the rope.

"I told you," McClain said, "you would never put a noose on my neck." A broad grin displayed his ugly yellow teeth. "I want you to sweat a minute before I blow your head off."

"If that gun goes off, you're a dead man, too," Blake said, his lips drawn thin.

"Whaddya mean?"

"Evidently you don't know much about Indians," Blake retorted. "How did you get all the way across the desert before?"

"Hitched onto a wagon train. Followed the stagecoach trail all the way from Eloy to Yuma."

"That explains a lot of things," Blake said. He had not moved a muscle. The rifle did not waver. "That Indian is not alone. There are others waiting for him to signal the attack. You fire that gun, they will come running."

McClain's brow showed worried furrows. "You're bluffin'," he said. "You just haven't got the guts to look death straight in the face." The little outlaw chuckled. "Go on, lawman. Sweat a little. This is your last day on earth. By afternoon, the buzzards will be pickin' your eyes out!"

The desert-wise sheriff knew that soon the Indians who waited for the leader's signal would know something was wrong. He must act quickly.

"Do you know what Apaches do, McClain?"

"Huh?"

"Torture is their specialty. To their savage minds, mercy is weakness. They will kill you slowly. When they start working on you, the noose in Tucson will look good to you!"

"Shut up!" McClain hissed. Blake noticed he was careful to keep his voice low.

"Not sure, eh?" queried Blake. "Apaches will cut off your arms while you're dying. They believe that by dismembering their enemies, they won't be able to harm them if they meet in the afterlife."

McClain swallowed hard. His sharp Adam's apple slid up and down his throat. "You're lying, Blake! You're buyin' time to breathe a little longer!"

"You sure don't know much about Indians," the kneeling sheriff said. "What are you going to do with your hands tied like that?"

"Say your prayers, tall man." McClain pulled his lip over a corner of his dirty teeth. "No noose for me."

The outlaw squeezed the trigger.

CHAPTER THREE

Sergeant Jed Cooley awakened at the first light of dawn. The wind that whipped through the shallow arroyo where he lay caused his big frame to shiver. He had given his blanket to one of the wounded men. Though he had slept soundly, he still felt weary.

His thoughts raced back over the previous day. He could see the waves of Apaches coming on painted horses. Once again he could hear their whooping, along with the heavy gunfire and the screams of wounded and dying men.

Suddenly he remembered. Lieutenant Taylor, lying in a thinly grooved gully, had raised his head to aim his revolver. The bullet struck him in the forehead. The back of his head was blown away.

The smell of hot coffee brewing brought him back to the present. Lifting his massive frame, he stood on his feet. Every muscle seemed to be tied in knots. Shaking himself and rubbing his thick neck, he walked to the steaming coffee pot.

"Good mornin'," Cooley said to the cook.

"Mornin', Sarge. Want some coffee?"

Nodding, Cooley picked up a cup and held it out. A few minutes later, sipping his coffee, he looked toward the east.

The sun had lifted its rim over the horizon, staining the sky a brilliant read.

Corporal Alex Todd, his right arm in a makeshift sling, approached the sergeant. Pointing westward with the tin cup in his left hand, Todd said, "See 'em, Sarge?"

Dozens of screeching buzzards were fighting among themselves while they picked meat from the dead Indian horses scattered on the desert floor.

"Samanti must have come for his dead during the night," observed Todd. "There's not a dead Indian out there."

Cooley was glancing toward the six wounded men who lay in a shallow arroyo, covered with blankets.

"How many of those savages did we kill, Sarge?"

"Close as I could figure, there were about thirty corpses layin' out there," the big man answered.

"Guess we're might lucky. There's still twenty-seven of us alive," Todd said.

"They'd have wiped us out if they hadn't run out of ammunition," Cooley said.

"Do you think they'll be back, Sarge?

"Not unless they have some ammunition stashed somewhere nearby. They'll need water, too."

Sergeant Cooley walked slowly to the arroyo where the six wounded men were being tended by Private Leonard Jenkins. Cooley admired this skinny little man. He watched over the wounded like a mother hen.

Jenkins had flunked out of medical school in Kansas City, but he had learned enough to be of considerable help to the wounded.

"When you've got a minute, I need to talk to you, Jenkins," said Cooley, walking past him.

"Be right with you, sir," Jenkins replied.

The sergeant heard Jenkins coming behind him. When they were out of earshot from the wounded men, Cooley turned and said, "We've got to move out in thirty minutes, Jenkins. Can those men ride?"

"I think five of them can, sir, but not Collins."

"Don't call me 'sir,' Jenkins. I'm only a sergeant," said Cooley.

"I'm sorry, sir…er…Sergeant. It's just…with the lieutenant dead, it seems I should call you 'sir.'"

"Save it for the next lieutenant," Cooley said. "You don't think Collins can ride?"

"The fever's got him, Sarge. The bullet is in his stomach. He won't last much longer."

"We'll have to leave him. I've got to get this platoon to water."

"But sir…I mean Sergeant, we can't leave him!"

"I'm sorry, Jenkins," Cooley said, his voice breaking, "we don't have any choice."

"I won't leave him!" the slender private said, raising his voice.

The ring of insubordination sounded in Cooley's ears. His face flushed with anger. His big neck tightened. In a flash, his hands gripped the little private's tattered shirt, lifting him off the ground. Holding him at eye level, Cooley shouted, "I've got this platoon to think of, Jenkins! The other wounded men need you! Who knows how many more of us will need you before this is over. Now get ready to move out!"

His anger abated by the outburst, the big man eased the little man down.

"I—I'm sorry, Sergeant. It's just that I can't bear the thought of leaving Collins here to die alone," Jenkins said, his lower lip quivering.

"I don't like it any more than you do, son, but we can't stay here. Indian Head Spring is more than a day's ride away. We have less than one day's supply of water. More men will die if we wait."

While the other wounded were being lifted onto their horses, Jenkins made a shelter from his own blanket and some mesquite branches. "This will keep the sun off of you," he said to the dying man.

As Jenkins walked to his horse, Sergeant Cooley knelt down beside Collins, whose body shook with fever, "You have your revolver, don't you, Collins?" the big man asked.

Collins dropped a quivering hand to his holster. Biting down on his chattering teeth, he nodded his head.

Tears filled Cooley's eyes. "I don't think the buzzards will bother you, but here's some extra cartridges, just in case."

Collins closed his eyes, swallowed hard, and nodded again.

"I hate to leave you, son, but I must get these men to water," said Cooley, trying to disguise his emotion.

"I—I understand," Collins said through thickened lips.

A slender shadow fell over Cooley's big frame. Jenkins knelt down. "Here's my canteen, Collins," he said, weeping. "It's over half full."

The dying man managed a smile. Leonard Jenkins sprang to his feet and hurried away. Cooley's big hand squeezed Collins' shoulder. "The Indians won't be back," Cooley said, "they've got to find water, too."

He stood up. With a dirty sleeve, he wiped away the tears. He paused a moment, looking at the long mound of dirt which marked the mass grave where the men who had died in yesterday's battle had been buried.

"Goodbye, Collins." Biting his lip, the big sergeant turned and shouted, "Mount up!" Swinging his leg over the saddle, his voice filled the desert air, "Forward, ho!" The column of men and horses moved out.

Several moments passed. The morning sun was getting hotter by the minute. The dust began to rise. Private Leonard Jenkins turned in the saddle. He could no longer see Collins, who lay in the shallow gully. The platoon moved to the northeast.

The sharp clap of the revolver echoed across the flat, dusty terrain. Jenkins gasped. The platoon stopped in unison as if a command had been given.

Sergeant Cooley said, "Smith, Hawley, Travers. Burial detail. We'll keep moving. Take an extra canteen. Catch up to us as soon as you can."

The rest of the platoon moved on.

The desert seemed to deplore the presence of man. Hot, dry, and foreboding, the vast expanse promised to destroy that alien mammal if he strayed within its bounds. It wasn't hard. The desert's arid fingers were skilled at seeking and drawing out the moisture in a man.

The sun was bearing down in full force as it continued to ride the morning sky. As the burial detail caught up with the platoon, the sergeant was stopping them to bury another one of the dead men. Working in brief shifts, the soldiers pitched dirt, sipped water, and wiped sweat.

The task finished, once again the voice of the big sergeant boomed, "Forward, ho!"

Corporal Alex Todd rode in the lead beside Sergeant Cooley. "Where do you suppose Samanti will go for water, Sarge?" he asked.

The big man turned in the saddle, unbuckled the strap on one of the saddlebags, and produced a worn, yellowed paper fragment. Unfolding it, he studied its contents. Corporal Todd recognized a map displaying the desert's terrain in detail.

Swaying with the rhythmic movement of his horse, Sergeant Cooley squinted against the glare produced by the map. "He'd have to cut north to the Gila River or make his way to Indian Head Spring. He'll go after ammunition. Hard to say where he might have that stashed."

The corporal watched the little rivers of sweat running through Cooley's red sideburns. "The big boy sure needs a shave," he thought to himself. He was running his palm over his own stubble when he caught Cooley's words.

"That stinkin' savage will come at us again, you can bet on that."

"Too bad we can't find him before he lays his hands on that ammunition," Todd interjected. "We could wipe out the whole bloodthirsty pack."

Sergeant Cooley reached in his shirt pocket and pulled out a soggy plug of tobacco. Biting off a chunk, he replaced the plug. He mumbled something inaudible to the corporal.

"What say, Sarge?" Todd asked.

Cooley rolled the brown mass to the other side of his mouth, spat a stream to the desert, and replied. "I said I want to kill that slimy snake with my bare hands. Shootin' the rest of them redskins is fine, but I want to bust Samanti's neck."

As the sun worked its way toward mid-sky, Private Leonard Jenkins rode directly behind Jed Cooley, listening to the men talking. Turning in the saddle to look at the four wounded men, Jenkins watched the dust rising from the pounding hooves. The platoon was covered with a thin film of slime, formed from a mixture of Arizona dust and human sweat. They looked like scarecrows with brown masks, revealing only red-rimmed eyes and parched lips.

Jenkins focused again on the wounded men. He wondered how much longer they could hold out. Thompson was nearly unconscious, swaying in the saddle like a broken tree limb in a strong wind. His left arm was shattered at the elbow.

Zimmerman had a bullet buried deep in his shoulder. Jenkins knew that removing it in these desert conditions would kill him instantly. Zimmerman would die, but at least the little private's care had given him a few more hours of life.

Wallace might make it. The bullet had gone clean through his side. If only they did not have to travel. The movement of the horse's body kept opening the wound. Wallace's trousers were soaked with blood.

Phil Runyon was in pretty bad shape. An Apache bullet

had ripped into his right thigh, shattering the bone. Jenkins feared gangrene. Sitting low in the saddle, Runyon grimaced in constant pain.

Straightening in his saddle, Jenkins stared at Jed Cooley's broad, muscular back, the sergeant's shirt soaked with sweat.

"We'll stop for water and rest in the canyon," Jenkins heard Cooley say. As Alex Todd stood up in the stirrups, squared his shoulders, and readjusted his sling, Jenkins lifted his gaze past Jed Cooley's back. Dancing in the distant heat waves, he saw the bare rock canyon looming toward the sky.

Two long plateaus stretched right and left to both horizons. Sometime in millenniums past, volcanic convulsions had torn the large plateau in two, leaving a sheer canyon of blistered rock. Boulders large and small were scattered about the entrance. Massive chunks of broken rock still supported teetering boulders high up on the canyon's crest, while others lay scattered along the canyon floor. Moving through the half-mile opening was a zigzag affair. Travelers had to go around giant boulders, their horses' hooves clattering on rocks, while at other times they pounded through soft dirt.

Jenkins wondered if a breeze might be moving in the canyon. He thought of how the night breeze had chilled him many hours ago. Hours? It seemed like days. He wanted to scream at the mocking desert and the restless sun. But it would only be a waste of strength.

One of the horses whinnied. Turning in the saddle, Jenkins saw Zimmerman fall. Leaping from his saddle as the platoon came to a halt, he knelt beside the fallen man. The slender private stood to his feet. Tears filled his eyes as

Sergeant Cooley rode toward him.

"He's dead, Sarge."

"Couple of you men put him on his horse," Cooley said. "We'll wait till after sundown to bury him. It'll be cooler then."

Leonard Jenkins helped the two men drape Zimmerman's body over his saddle. Running a piece of rope through the dead man's belt, he cinched it to the saddle horn.

Zimmerman's arms and legs swayed freely with the horse's movements as the platoon moved toward the jutting canyon. When they were about a half-mile from the rock-strewn entrance, Sergeant Cooley lifted his hand, signaling the group to halt.

"Smith! Palmer! Scout it out!"

The two horses lifted a cloud of brown dust as they trotted ahead. Cooley slung his arm forward. The platoon moved slowly toward the canyon.

"Do you think Samanti might plan an ambush, Sarge?" Alex Todd asked in a nervous tone.

"Not unless he's picked up some ammunition. He can't be too far ahead of us, if he's going our way. The only tracks I've seen are at least two or three days old."

"Is there another way he could get on the other side of the plateau?"

Producing a map again, Cooley examined it closely. After several minutes, he said, "Looks like he would have to go at least a day's ride south to do it. Unless there are some passages that are not shown on the map."

Smith and Palmer were disappearing into the deep shade

of the canyon's mouth. Every soldier watched and waited as they plodded forward. Time seemed to drag. Jed Cooley removed his hat, revealing a wet mop of red hair. With a slimy sleeve, he wiped the mud from his brow.

The two scouts emerged back into the sunlight. Smith swung his arm in a circular motion, beckoning the platoon toward the canyon.

Jenkins' curiosity about breezes in the canyon was soon answered.

Moving past the hot rocks strewn at the entrance, the weary men imagined that they were riding into an overheated oven. Out of the direct rays of the sun, the air was close and stifling.

Private Smith pointed to the soft earth on the canyon floor. "Samanti hasn't been through here, Sarge," he said, "these tracks are at least a week old and the horses were shod."

Nodding his head in acknowledgement, Cooley lifted his voice, "We'll rest at the other end of the canyon, men."

The half-mile seemed like a hundred. Even the horses displayed their dislike for the stifling, motionless air. At last came the command to dismount. Stopping just inside the rock walls, the weary men watered their horses, while Leonard Jenkins tended to the wounded.

Tenderly, Jenkins worked on their bandages. Private Thompson was nauseated, writhing in the throes of the dry heaves. Wallace grimaced as Jenkins cinched up his bandage, trying to put a stop to the oozing blood.

The slender man's face turned a livid white when he examined Phil Runyon's leg. It was gangrenous. Through clenched teeth, Runyon sputtered, "I can't go on, Len! Just leave me here!"

Lifting a canteen to Runyon's lips, Jenkins forced an encouraging tone into his voice. "A little rest and you'll feel better, Phil." Runyon was dying. Both men knew it.

It sounded like thunder at first.

The horses jumped and bolted for open space, their eyes wild. Lifting his eyes upward, Sergeant Cooley saw the giant boulder rocking its way downward.

"Look out!" his voice bellowed, as he jerked men to their feet. The boulder was breaking rocks and dirt loose as it thundered downward, loosing an avalanche upon the entrance.

Men and horses were scattering for daylight in the midst of the deafening roar. When Sergeant Cooley was in the clear, he spun around to see if anyone was under the avalanche. Something high up caught his eye. Against the azure canopy overhead, he saw movement of near-naked bronzed bodies. Quickly they disappeared from the cliff's edge.

"Samanti!"

The roar stopped as quickly as it had started. A thick cloud of dust covered the canyon's entrance, rising full-length to the top. Men were coughing, spitting, cursing.

A quick survey revealed nineteen men and twenty-three horses remaining. "We were mighty lucky, Sarge," Corporal Todd said. "The pack horses were nearest to the entrance. We've still got our water!"

Sergeant Cooley was staring toward the massive pile of rubble. "Jenkins! Where's Jenkins?"

"He didn't make it, Sarge," one of the men ejaculated.

"I saw him, Sarge," cried another. "He flung himself over Runyon!"

Cooley's big frame shook. His fists were clenched. His eyes filled with tears. "Poor kid," he said, "never thought of himself…"

He spun on his heels and ran about fifty yards. Stopping suddenly, he turned around, beat on his chest, and let out a savage yell that carried to the canyon's mouth and reverberated off the rock walls. For several moments he stood there rigid and motionless. Eighteen men stood in silence. They waited. They watched.

The big man sauntered toward the group, his broad shoulders swaying like a tall tree in the wind. Stopping about ten paces from the group, Cooley stuck both arms straight out. Curling his fingers into claws, he spoke with emotion. "These hands will kill that stinkin' savage! I swear it! Do you hear me? I'll kill him with my bare hands!"

Stiff-legged, he walked to his horse. "Mount up!" Pointing his horses' face to the northeast, he shouted, "Forward, ho!"

The familiar cloud of dust enveloped them once again. Corporal Alex Todd was watching the big sergeant out of the corner of his eye. He was looking straight ahead, seeing nothing.

Todd took note that the face of the desert was slowly changing as they moved northeastward. The blistering rocks were always present. It seemed to the corporal that the rocks, in retaliation, were throwing the heat back at the sun. Cholla cactus, mingled amongst the wand-like ocotillos, was more prevalent on this side of the rock canyon. Countless yucca plants, with their stiff leaves and white flowers, dotted the land.

An unrecognizable little desert animal skittered across the trail. A large lizard sunned itself on a flat rock. The only sounds were the soft clopping of hooves, squeaking saddles, and the occasional blow of a horse.

Samanti and his bronzed companions watched the platoon moving away in a cloud of reddish-brown dust. There was a breeze high up on the canyon's rim. None of the Apaches relished the descent to the burning desert floor.

Standing on a tall rock with his long black hair flowing in the breeze, the renegade leader made a grotesque sight. Silhouetted against the desert sky, he resembled a bronzed statue. He was every inch an Indian from his thin humped nose and high cheekbones to his swift and silent moccasined feet.

Tall and slender, Samanti wore a silver star on a leather thong around his neck and the typical gold armbands on his arms just above his biceps. On his waist, he wore a sharp bone-handled knife. His ability with the knife was both feared and respected all over the southwest. He was brutal in hand-to-hand combat and deadly in a throwing contest.

The renegade leader spoke to his lieutenant, Hondo. "We must get to the spring ahead of white eyes. Yellow Fang will have ammunition. White eyes' troops must die!"

"Then we must travel at night, Samanti," said Hondo. "This is not good."

"Sometimes Indian fears and traditions must be ignored," Samanti said. "Let us go."

Samanti's remaining fifty-eight men descended the hidden trail to the burning desert floor. Tethered in an open area surrounded by tall rock formations were over seventy horses, including ten pack horses carrying ample water. The army platoon had never seen the pack horses.

Although this arid land had been their habitat most of their lives, the Apaches also felt the unfriendliness of the desert. The blazing sun, the burning sand, the prickly cactus, the ever-present dust, all united to remind the Indian that he, too, was an invader.

Samanti's band followed the path of the U.S. Army platoon. They kept a safe distance, knowing that when the white men camped, they would keep moving toward Indian Head Spring. Samanti nurtured a deep hope that Yellow Fang and his warriors would be waiting at the spring. They would have ammunition. Working together, the Yaquis and Apaches would ambush the platoon and massacre them.

As the dust lifted on their bronzed bodies, the Apache renegades endured the desert's torturous heat. Conversation was sometimes in Spanish, sometimes in Apache, with an occasional English word. Altogether, it was at a minimum.

Samanti nursed his vengeful hatred for the whites with quiet and bitter memories. He thought of the great hunting grounds to the north. He remembered the old men telling of the days when the Indians had the run of the country. They were free to ride the wind without interference. This was their land. And then came the cursed white man with his lies and greed.

Seething with burning hatred, he thought of the pact he had made with Yellow Fang. "White Eyes will be punished," they agreed. Suddenly into his mind's eye came the face of Gray Wolf. For a moment he smiled, forgetting his hatred for the whites. How great was his love for the stalwart Yaqui brave. The flame of hatred resurfaced when he remembered his last words to Gray Wolf, "Someday we will have revenge on the white man together!"

Samanti's heart throbbed with excitement. The sweet thought of revenge eased the heat of the burning sun.

Hondo's voice broke the silence. "We will need rest, Samanti," he was saying. "How long will we travel after darkness falls?"

"We will mark when soldiers make camp, then ride for maybe three hours. If we leave tomorrow at dawn, we will stay plenty far ahead. We must reach Spring before army."

Hondo nodded in agreement.

The sun's persistent rays continued to draw moisture from man and beast. "We must stop for water," said Samanti. Glad for the respite from the endless walking, the horses sucked eagerly at the water. Samanti's men gulped the colorless liquid, shaking the tormenting thirst.

A pair of vultures watched the Apaches from a tall rock. Samanti lifted himself to his horse's back. Staring for a moment at the vultures, he spoke to them. "Follow us, amigos! We will provide you with white flesh to fill your hungry stomachs!" The savages whooped with excitement at their leader's words and lifted dust as they moved on.

CHAPTER FOUR

s Talking Rifle lay dead with his face in the sand, Duke McClain steadied the muzzle of the Indian's rifle between Sheriff Matt Blake's eyes and squeezed the trigger.

The gun did not fire.

McClain jerked at the lever. Glancing upward, he saw the tall form silhouetted against the gray sky. The barrel of Blake's .45 cracked against the side of his head. Crouching low, Blake lifted the Winchester from the unconscious outlaw's limp fingers. Dropping the lever, he looked into the empty chamber. "Sure glad for cautious Indians," he said under his breath. Snapping the lever back in place, he cocked the cartridge into the chamber.

Picking up his own rifle, he made his way across the arroyo and slipped on his boots. Those Indians out there would be getting edgy by now. He peered over the south rock wall at a low spot. His eye caught the movement. An Indian was crawling toward him. Figuring to empty the dead Indian's rifle first, he lifted it. The crawling red man, curious to know what was happening behind the rocks, was coming fast. He was within twenty yards. Blake knew there had to be others. He could wait no longer.

Sighting at the Indian's head, the rifle bucked in his hands. The man made no sound. Blake knew he had not missed. He quickly ejected the spent shell, filling the chamber.

An Indian stepped around the west opening of the arroyo. Before he could level his rifle, the sheriff put a bullet through his heart. Figuring the next move would come through the opposite opening, Matt Blake flattened himself on the ground at the base of the south rock wall and waited.

The horses were moving about with their hind legs, trying to pull loose from their tethers. Watching both entrances while keeping an eye on the walls, Blake swallowed hard. How many were out there? Could he hold them off, or was McClain right? Maybe the buzzards would have his eyes for supper. Was there some kind of twisted fate that would keep him from seeing the noose around McClain's scrawny neck? The Indians would kill Duke for sure. Probably torture him first. But that wouldn't be right. McClain's sins were against white men. He should die the white man's way. The noose.

The big dun snorted and whinnied. The Indian came over the north wall like an antelope. He fired at the prostrate sheriff. The bullet splattered rock fragments and ricocheted angrily. Blake shot him through the midsection. The Indian lived long enough to give a faint cry, stagger three steps, and fall. His blood made a pool, which in moments was sucked away by the thirsty sand, leaving a brown spot.

All was quiet. The horses settled down. Somewhat encouraged, the Tucson lawman picked up his hat from where it lay beside his saddle and wiping the sweat from his brow, put it on. Bellying down, he crawled to the east opening, carrying both rifles. The sun was bearing down on the desert now. Looking out across the dust and sand, he could see no movement.

Within half an hour, Blake had completed the circle. If there were other Indians, they had gone, he told himself. McClain was beginning to stir. There was blood on his face and in his hair.

After moving the three corpses to the north rock wall, Blake watered and fed the horses. McClain was awake, now moaning with pain. His eyes were filled with fire. He cursed the sheriff, calling Blake some names even the lawman had not heard.

"I told you...you don't know much about Indians, Duke. When they are moving and don't want to be detected, they leave the chamber empty. Don't want to discharge the gun by accident."

"There'll be a next time," McClain said with clenched yellow teeth. "I'm gonna kill you, Blake. You hear?"

Ignoring McClain's threat, Blake built a dry, nearly smokeless fire. The two men ate hard biscuits and beef jerky while they drank coffee. A pair of buzzards passed overhead, screeching.

"Blake, those ropes are killin' my wrists," the hook-nosed outlaw said. "How about a little relief?"

"I'll loosen them when it snows in Panama...or we get to Tucson, whichever comes first," the tall lawman said with a tight smile.

After cleaning the cooking utensils, Blake saddled the

horses and loaded the pack on the roan. "Let's go," he said.

Suddenly, McClain moved toward his horse. As Blake stepped into the stirrups and raised himself upward, his eyes caught a movement over the south wall. Dropping to his feet, he whispered, "Hold it! Don't get on your horse!"

McClain rubbed his aching head and watched as the sheriff crouched at the east opening and looked southward. "What is it, Blake?"

"Indians! Two of them are dragging the body of one I shot this morning. Looks like they're trying to work around to the north."

Blake was puzzled. If there were more around, why hadn't they attacked? He watched the two braves strain against the dead man's weight. Suddenly one of them collapsed. The other one tried to help him. Soon, he also fell to the earth. The latter struggled to his feet and fell again.

The sun bore down with invisible flaming torrents. The two savages were barely moving. "They're in bad shape," Blake said to himself. Turning to McClain, he said, "Just as well sit down. Looks like we're going to be here awhile."

Gray Wolf lay flat on the crest of the butte, observing his two braves struggling with the corpse. He had watched two buzzards swoop low over the dead brave several times. He knew when they were sure he was dead, they would tear the flesh from the bones.

Indians have a sacred reverence for the mortal body. They believe any damage done to it in death will result in the same damage in the after-life. They will risk their lives to care for their dead. The two braves writhing in the heat, making themselves vulnerable targets, were proof of this.

Gray Wolf knew from the silence that had prevailed from the rock-walled arroyo since the gunfire had ceased that Talking Rifle and the others were dead. If they had killed the two white riders, they would have returned by now.

The muscular Yaqui looked back at the five men lying a few yards below him. The heat was taking its toll. Their strength was gone. They were losing their will to live. Quiet Bear looked up at Gray Wolf. "We must have water, Gray Wolf. We must have it now!" The Yaqui leader knew that death was hovering near.

"If we only had ammunition!" Gray Wolf exclaimed. "We don't stand a chance against the whites without our guns. We have no strength to fight them with our knives."

Gray Wolf closed his eyes and rolled on his back. The sun bore down with murderous heat. If felt as though hot metal spikes were being jabbed into his eyelids. Laying his arm across his eyes to shield against the sun's relentless rays, he tried to think. What could he do for those dying men…and himself?

From out on the flat he could hear the weak voice of one of the bucks who had gone after the corpse. "Water! Water! Water!"

From below him, Gray Wolf heard a muffled cry. Sitting up, he saw one of the braves, face down in the dust. Rushing to him, he turned him over. The man's own knife was buried in his stomach, up to the hilt. He had chosen this way of death, rather than the slow, torturous death by thirst.

Gray Wolf sobbed as he tenderly pulled the knife from the dead man's stomach.

Matt Blake got to his feet. Straining his ears, he heard it again. One of the Indians lying out there with the corpse was begging for water. He squinted his eyes against the glare. Both men were still down. They had been in the same spot for some time.

McClain stepped up beside him. "It's a dirty Indian trick, Blake," the little man said. "They want to lure us out there and kill us!"

"I don't think so," replied the sheriff. "Something's wrong. Those two were dragging that body somewhere. There's got to be more Indians out there. I keep asking myself, 'Why didn't the whole bunch come here after us?'"

The pitiful cry for water came again.

Blake went on. "They're out of ammunition and they're out of water. These are not Apaches."

"Not Apaches!" McClain said with a surprised look.

"No. They're Yaquis. From up north. I don't know what they are doing here, but it's evident they are not acquainted with this country. They probably expected water holes to be more plentiful, like in the north."

Blake walked to his horse and lifted a canteen strap from the pommel. He pulled his rifle from the scabbard.

"What are you doin'?" McClain asked, with acid in his tone. "You ain't gonna take our water to them dirty savages!"

"No. You are," answered the sheriff.

"Me?"

"Yeah. You." Blake placed the canteen in the outlaw's closely knit hands. "Those are human beings out there and as long as we've got water, we can't let them die of thirst."

"You're crazy!" bellowed McClain.

"You want a lump on the other side of your head?" Blake asked, frowning down at the little man.

McClain did not answer. Together they walked toward the Yaquis lying on the burning earth. As they drew near, the sheriff held his rifle ready. His hands relaxed on the gun when he beheld them. Their faces were virtual death masks.

Kneeling down, Blake took the canteen from Duke McClain. With the rifle held in the crook of his arm, he lifted the head of one Indian, then that of the other, intermittently. He poured small amounts into their mouths, giving them time to swallow and accustom their throats to moisture once again. One of the braves opened his eyes and focused them on the sheriff's weather-worn face. He ran his tongue over his swollen upper lip and smiled.

"Gray Wolf!" Quiet Bear was standing on the crest of the butte. "Come look!"

The Yaqui leader scrambled to his feet, leaving the dead brave. He shaded his eyes with his hand.

"The white men are giving water to Tall Tree and Red Bird!" Quiet Bear shouted. The other Indians struggled to their feet. With effort they made their way to the crest to stand with Gray Wolf and Quiet Bear.

Gray Wolf ran his dry tongue over his cracked lips. The tall man was waving to them. "He is telling us to come to him!" cried Quiet Bear.

The thirst-crazed Yaquis found themselves running toward the tall man. They stumbled and fell, rolled in the dust, and clambered to their feet again…running, stumbling. As they approached the tall man, they saw that Tall Tree and Red Bird were now sitting up.

Tall Tree had pointed out the muscular Gray Wolf as their leader. Matt Blake extended the canteen to Gray Wolf. The gallant Indian refused, saying that his men would drink first. As it passed from man to man, Gray Wolf said, "Take only small swallows, my brothers, or you will become very sick."

As Gray Wolf was downing his share, Matt Blake said, "Tall Tree, here, said there were six of you on the butte. I count only five."

Wiping his mouth with the back of his hand, Gray Wolf said, "One of our braves just chose a quick death. I wonder that any of us are still alive. As soon as we have strength, we must bury our dead."

As Gray Wolf handed the empty canteen back to the sheriff, he noticed the ropes on McClain's wrists. The outlaw stared at him coldly.

"I am Sheriff Matt Blake out of Tucson. This man is my prisoner. I am taking him back to Tucson to stand trial for murder."

"You'll never do it now, you fool!" McClain blurted out. "These savages will kill us both!"

Ignoring the outburst, the Yaqui leader extended a muscular right arm. "I am Gray Wolf of the Yaqui nation."

Blake and Gray Wolf shook hands Indian style. Gray Wolf smiled. "You are blood brother of Yaquis," he said in deep earnest. "You have saved our lives. I must make apology for attack on you this morning."

For years, Matt Blake had detested the government's handling of the Indians. He knew their feelings for the white man had a justifiable basis. Gray Wolf and his men would have no reason to believe that the two white riders would willingly share their water.

"I understand," replied Blake, placing his hand on his new "blood brother's" shoulder. Pointing with the other hand to the rock entrance, he said, "We have more water. We will leave you some." The group followed as Blake and Gray Wolf walked side by side toward the arroyo. McClain remained aloof.

"Do you have food?" the tall man asked.

"A little," came the answer.

"We'll give you some of ours," Blake said. "We're heading for Indian Head Spring. We'll find game there."

Gray Wolf wondered if he should tell the white man of his rendezvous with Samanti at Indian Head Spring. He pondered on it as they stepped into the rock-enclosed arroyo. His eyes fastened on the three corpses lying next to the rock wall. "This white man is a good fighter," he thought to himself.

Blake was lifting canteens from his horse. "We are also going to Indian Head Spring," Gray Wolf said. "We are to meet friends there."

Dropping the straps back over the pommel, Blake said, "Good. Then we will travel together." He opened the saddlebag. Reaching inside, he fumbled past the curry comb. Lying right next to McClain's Remington .44 was a neatly wrapped package of beef jerky. Leaving the strap unbuckled for the anticipated return of the package, he then removed some hardtack from the pack horse. "You and your men will eat now and drink some more water. I will help you bury your dead and we will be on our way. What about your horses?"

"They are also nearly dead," replied Gray Wolf. "We have grain for them. But they need water."

"We are only half a day from the Spring," Blake said. "I think we can give them enough to make it to the Spring. There will be plenty of water for all, then."

The Indians wolfed down the jerky and hardtack between sips of the life-giving water. Gray Wolf felt the strength oozing back into his muscular body. He looked at Matt Blake, who was peeling off some more jerky. The sheriff never thought he would read affection for himself in an Indian's eyes, but it was there, clearly, unmistakably. The Yaqui leader's words seemed to echo in Blake's mind as he looked into those dark eyes. "You are blood brother of Yaquis. You saved our lives."

Sheriff Blake had noticed McClain roll a cigarette and walk to the east opening of the arroyo, blowing smoke into the hot desert air. Busied with caring for the Indians, he did not notice the little man casually making his way between the pack horse and the dun. The strap on the saddlebag was still unbuckled. He glanced in the direction of Blake. Gray Wolf was explaining the rendezvous with Samanti and promising safety for the two white men. Blake's back was toward him.

McClain lifted his rope-laced wrists and dipped his hands into the saddlebag. Fumbling for a moment, he felt the smooth barrel of his revolver. In a moment he had the butt in his right hand. He looked around the horse's rump toward the sheriff. Blake was still hunkered down with his back to the outlaw. McClain untied the reins of Blake's horse.

He stepped into the open and leveled the gun at Blake. With the cigarette dangling from the corner of his mouth, he spoke coldly. "On your feet, Blake!"

The sheriff stood up to his full height. The circular end of the muzzle looked like a single menacing eye. "You!" McClain shouted at Gray Wolf. "Turn the dun around. He's already untied!"

Gray Wolf led the horse in a circular motion. "Bring him right here," the outlaw commanded, motioning with his head. Knowing it would take him a few seconds to get in the saddle with his hands tied together, McClain said to Gray Wolf, "Now get over there by the stinkin' lawman."

Gray Wolf eyed him cautiously, slowly moving to stand by Blake. The other six Yaquis were still sitting on the ground, holding food in their hands, but no longer eating.

"Now, mister tall man, you drop your gun belt," McClain commanded. The outlaw's plan was to put the horse between himself and the sheriff, keeping the gun on him while he worked his way into the saddle. Once mounted, he would blow Blake into eternity, shoot Gray Wolf, and ride the swift horse to freedom.

Blake had not moved. The dun was standing with his nose just to McClain's right. He dared not move any further with his plan until that gun belt was on the ground. The Tucson sheriff was lightning with a gun.

Nervously he shouted, his narrow eyes flashing fire, "I said drop that gun belt!" McClain thumbed back the hammer. With a double click, the cylinder turned. "Drop it!" the outlaw yelled.

Blake opened his mouth to say something when, like a cougar, Gray Wolf sprang forward. The hammer slammed forward with a hollow "click." The powerful Gray Wolf flattened McClain with a body blow. The wiry little man swung the barrel at the Indian's head... Ducking the swing, Gray Wolf brought an uppercut from the ground. With a crackling crunch, McClain went down. Shaking his head, the outlaw raised the gun, pointing it into Gray Wolf's face. It clicked again.

As Gray Wolf lunged, he pulled his knife.

"No! Gray Wolf! No!" shouted Blake, springing forward to stay the angry Indian's hand. "I must have him alive!"

Slowly, Gray Wolf sheathed his knife and stood up. Looking down at the little outlaw who still gripped the .44, he said, "Matt Blake is Gray Wolf's blood brother. To threaten him is to threaten Gray Wolf. You live only because blood brother wishes it so."

Blake leaned over, taking the revolver from Duke McClain's now-limp fingers. "I forgot to tell you, Duke. I removed the cartridges. Guess you are getting' edgy, though. You haven't killed anybody in several days. That must be rough on a mad dog."

McClain snarled as Blake placed the revolver back into the saddlebag. "We will water your horses, now. Then we will bury your dead," Blake said to Gray Wolf.

The sun was past the halfway point in the morning sky as the seven Indians and two white men rode away from the rock-mounded graves.

A cloud of dust lifted toward the sky, leaving portions of itself on the men and horses. To the Indians, somehow the dust was not as bothersome as it had seemed before. The moisture in their mouths, the food in their stomachs, made the whole desert look better.

Sheriff Matt Blake scanned the country around him with narrowed eyes. This was familiar territory. He had been through here before. Some twenty-five miles north was the Gila River, washing its banks day and night. Drawing its crystal clear waters from the mountain streams of western New Mexico, it wended its way in a southwesterly direction across southern Arizona. At Yuma, it joined forces with the waters of the mighty Colorado River to flow due south through the northern tip of the Baja California desert in Mexico, to empty out in the Gulf of California.

Twenty miles to the south was Mexico's border. From there the Mexican "banditos" came to prey on travelers in southern Arizona. Plundering and killing, they often scalped their victims to throw the blame on the Apaches. Needless to say, the Apaches held no love for the Mexicans.

Spotting a formation of tall red rocks about three miles ahead, Matt Blake said to himself, "I want just a few minutes to stop at the grave."

Neglecting his thoughts for a moment, Blake pointed forward and spoke to Gray Wolf. "We will stop for a rest and water at those tall rocks." The Indian spoke a word of acknowledgement. Gazing at the distant rocks lifting their heads toward the azure curtain above, the lawman went back to his thoughts.

He swallowed hard as he thought of the young deputy. Danny O'Toole seemed destined to go down in American history with the great names of such lawmen as Wyatt Earp, Pat Garrett, and Ben Johnson. A Mexican bullet altered his destiny.

As Blake's deputy, he had sought and apprehended many notorious outlaws. It was he who had trailed the infamous Chancy brothers to the little border town of San Salto, south of Yuma. The four outlaws had held up two banks in Tucson on the same day, killing a bank teller and a customer. Sheriff Matt Blake was on his way to Phoenix on business. The twenty-four-year-old O'Toole left another deputy in charge of the Tucson office and trailed the killers to San Salto. He went to the town marshal for help in arresting the Chancys and found him sleeping off a drunk in his office. He decided to ask for help from some of the citizens. Walking up San Salto's only street, he headed for the barber shop. The barber always knew all the men of the town.

Suddenly the four outlaws stepped out from a doorway and faced him. Matt Blake had taught him how to draw, shoot, and fight.

"You gonna draw on all four of us, sonny boy?" sneered Bud Chancy.

"Better take your little toy star and go home, little feller," chimed in Luke.

"All four of you are under arrest for murder," Danny O'Toole said.

Mel Chancy looked toward the cloudless blue sky and clucked his tongue three times against the roof of his mouth. "You sure picked a nice day to die, deputy!"

"Yeah," added Jack, "September twenty-second will look good on yer grave marker."

Luke went for the gun first. He died first. The bullet tore through his heart. He was dead before he hit the ground. Bud and Mel had not even cleared leather before Jack was on his way down. While the blue smoke drifted away from the muzzle of O'Toole's gun, the two remaining Chancys lifted their hands high over their heads.

Draping the bodies of the two dead Chancy brothers over their horses, Deputy O'Toole took all four to Yuma. There he telegraphed Blake in Phoenix to come help him return the remaining Chancy brothers to Tucson.

Matt Blake felt a faint smile tug at the corners of his mouth. He thought of Jack Chancy's choice words of September twenty-second looking good on a grave marker. That was the exact date carved on the marker over his grave in Yuma's somber graveyard.

They were approaching the tall red rocks. "We'll haul up here and water the horses," Blake said to Gray Wolf. Dismounting, the tall man felt a pang of sorrow shoot through his heart. This was where it had happened. He stared at the rocks. They magnified the bitter memory.

The four of them, Bud Chancy, Mel Chancy, Danny O'Toole, and himself, were just coming abreast of the rocks, when seven Mexican banditos stepped out from the rocks and leveled rifles at them.

"Ho, gringos," the fat leader said, "stop right there!" Blake remembered the silver-studded double bandoliers that criss-crossed his fat chest. His swarthy skin emphasized his big white teeth when he smiled and said, "Your money, please!"

Blake remembered how he was explaining that they were just lawmen taking their prisoners to Tucson, when Mel Chancy butted in. "Hey, amigo! My brother and me have a lot of money stashed near Yuma. If you'll kill these two lawmen and set us free, we'll take you to the money and split it with you!"

The fat Mexican smiled broadly. "How much you got, gringo?"

"Over forty thousand," Mel answered, smiling weakly.

The rotund bandito turned and motioned for his men to gather around him. They spoke in Spanish, four or five speaking at once. Blake remembered turning to Mel Chancy, saying, "When you give them their split, they'll kill you for the rest of it. Even if you give it to them, they'll kill you anyhow. Killing is their main pleasure."

"If we went on with you, we'd hang, wouldn't we?" snapped Bud.

"Yeah, we'll take our chances with the Mex!" Mel retorted.

The dark-skinned men were still talking. "Matt, we better make our break right now while they're huddled together. It's our only chance," Danny O'Toole said in a low voice. Blake nodded.

Just as both Chancy brothers started to shout a warning to the clustered Mexicans, both lawmen gouged their spurs into horseflesh. The horses bolted, charging straight for the huddle. Both six-guns were firing, striking Mexican flesh. The first one to raise his rifle caught a bullet in the chest. The gun discharged with a slight waver, sending the bullet into Mel Chancy's stomach, knocking him from the saddle.

Mexicans were rolling in the dust from the impact of the two bolting horses. Both lawmen spun their horses around, firing and charging again. Two of them were back on their feet, blazing away at the charging lawmen. Out of the corner of his eye, Blake saw Danny's horse go down. Putting a bullet in one of the standing men and hitting the other one with his horse, Blake spun his horse around again. Danny was lying prostrate on the ground, unloading his gun into the dusty pile of Mexicans. Two of them were blasting away at him while he was trying to reload. Blake, realizing his own gun was empty, spurred his horse and ran down the two who were firing at Danny. Holstering his Colt, he yanked the Winchester repeater from the saddle scabbard.

Only two Mexicans were stirring. One was throwing down an empty rifle, searching for his pistol. The other was firing at Blake. He felt a searing bolt of fire in his left shoulder as he fired the Winchester from the hip. While the swarthy man went down, Blake cocked his rifle and drove a bullet through the last man's heart.

He could feel the blood running down his left arm as he dismounted. He paused for a moment, looking over the bodies of the banditos. The fat leader lay on his back, his sightless eyes staring upward. There was a blue hole on the left side of his forehead. Making sure they were all dead, Blake ran to Danny. A rifle bullet had struck him through the right eye.

Matt Blake had carried Danny O'Toole's body to the base of the tall rocks before he began to think clearly. There lay the body of Mel Chancy. Bud! He was gone. In the middle of the dust and gunsmoke, he had hightailed it for freedom, leaving his dying brother on the ground…

Coming back to the present, Matthew Blake found himself standing over the mound of small rocks. The grave lay in the shadow of the tall rocks, as far out of sight as Matt Blake could put it. He had no tools with which to dig. He had scooped out a place in the dust about eight inches deep with his bare hands, all the while with blood oozing from the flesh wound in his shoulder.

Wrapping Danny's body in saddle blankets from the Mexican horses, he placed it in the shallow grave and covered it with rocks about four feet deep.

Seven years had passed. Standing over the grave, it suddenly seemed like yesterday. Tears filled his eyes. "You were the best, Danny," he said. "The very best."

While wiping the tears with his dusty shirt sleeve, he became aware of another presence.

"You all right, my brother?" Gray Wolf was asking from behind him.

"Yes, my brother," Blake said, turning to face the Yaqui. "Just reliving some old memories."

"This is a grave?"

"Yes. We'd better get going now. I will tell you about it as we ride."

Walking together around the rock formation, the pair climbed onto their horses. Once again they were on their way toward Indian Head Spring. The tall man looked back one time.

While the dust rose around them, Matt Blake told Gray Wolf the story he had just relived. "I left the other bodies to the beasts and buzzards," he told Gray Wolf. "With my shoulder bleeding, I couldn't bury them."

The Indian riding beside him nodded. "What about Bud Chancy?"

"Well, I knew the Mexican horses would drift back to their homeland, so I took Mel's horse with me and lit out after him. My wound was only superficial. I knew it would be all right once I had cleaned it and got the bleeding stopped."

The sheriff lifted his hat, mopped his brow, and continued. "I tracked him back to where they had buried the money under a clump of bushes among some hills just east of San Salto. He was digging like crazy and cussing up a storm when I rode up on him."

Matt Blake threw his head back and laughed.

"What is so funny?" queried Gray Wolf.

"You should have seen his face when I told him that Danny had tracked them there and dug up the money. I had it right there in my saddlebag!"

Gray Wolf laughed. It struck Blake that he had never heard an Indian laugh.

"You took him back to Tucson?" the Indian asked, still chuckling.

"Yes. He stood trial and was convicted. We hung him." Blake turned in the saddle to see if Duke McClain had been listening. He had.

"I still say there'll be a different story this time, lawman," he said, fixing his cold glare on the sheriff's blue eyes. Turning his head, he spit in the dust.

Straightening up in the saddle, Blake noticed the wagon tracks, just like those he had seen earlier. There definitely were two wagons. One rider rode alongside the wagons. He figured the travelers were about a day ahead of them.

The day rolled on. Twice again, they stopped for rest and water. Moving once more, Blake took note that the sun was tilting downward in the southwestern sky. Unmitigating in its torment, the fiery mass in the sky continued to warp the moisture from his lanky body.

He thought about his predicament. Gray Wolf was to meet Samanti at the spring. Samanti was thirsty for white man's blood. Would Gray Wolf be able to handle the wild Apache? The two Indians were friends, but just how far would that relationship stretch?

And then there was Duke McClain. Even if Gray Wolf could persuade Samanti to spare the sheriff's life...what about his prisoner? It was he who had saved the Yaquis' lives, not McClain. For that matter, the yellow-haired little man had shown hostility toward the Yaquis. He even tried to blow Gray Wolf's head off. Put in a tight place, Gray Wolf just might let McClain die.

Every inch a lawman, Matt Blake knew he would have to put his own life on the line to save the sleazy little killer. There was a noose waiting in Tucson. Whatever it cost Blake, "Mad-dog" must hang at the hands of white men for his crimes.

Then, of course, there was McClain himself. The Tucson

lawman made this trek before with a prisoner, but Bud Chancy was a lamb compared with McClain. Chancy and his brothers only killed when spurred by their lustful greed. Duke McClain killed for the sheer thrill of killing. Taking a human life meant no more to him than stepping on a bug.

The wary sheriff knew he would have to be on constant guard all the way to Tucson. Twice this very day the outlaw had tried to kill him. The first time, McClain's ignorance of Indian caution had spared him. The second time, his own carefulness had done it. There could be no slackening of caution for a moment.

Suddenly his brain registered to his consciousness what his eyes were seeing. On the horizon, at the crest of a long, gentle rise, was the giant rock resembling the shape and profile of an Indian's head.

"There it is!" he exclaimed, pointing toward the horizon. The Yaquis, who had been silent most of the way, began to talk among themselves. Blake did not understand the Yaqui lingo, but several times his dust-filled ears caught the word "Samanti."

An icy hand seemed to close its fingers around his heart.

CHAPTER FIVE

Rod Chamberlain and Will Nichols cringed as they rode past the Yuma Territorial Prison. The famous penal institution was situated on the south bank of the Gila River atop a barren bluff. Nichols stared for several moments at the ugly brown adobe buildings, the dismal walls, and the foreboding gates of heavy timber.

"They'll never put me in that place, Rob," he said with a shudder. "I'll go out with my gun blazing, but they'll not put me in a place like that!"

"Play it smart and that'll never be your worry," retorted the other outlaw.

The sun was leaning low in the western sky as they rode into Yuma.

After robbing the bank at Blanding, the duo had to hole up in a cave, hiding from the angry posse. After two days, they headed southwest toward Flagstaff. Although they were behind schedule for their rendezvous with Duke McClain in Yuma, they took the time to rob one of Flagstaff's two banks. Again, they drew a posse.

The posse waylaid them in Chino Valley. A fierce gun battle

ensued, in which they had used up most of their ammunition. Under cover of darkness they finally eluded the posse.

Arriving in Kirkland Junction just before dawn, they broke into the town's only gun shop and replenished their ammunition supply. By the time the proprietor had discovered his loss, they were many miles away.

They were now arriving in Yuma three days late. "You don't suppose Duke got nervous and lit out, do you?" Nichols said.

"We'll soon find out," Chamberlain answered.

Duke McClain, having never been to Yuma, told his two partners to check at the hotels if they arrived in daylight hours and at the saloons if they came in at night.

Reining up in front of the Sundeen Hotel, Chamberlain said, "There's still about an hour of daylight left. Let's start with the hotels. What was the name he'd use?"

"Richard Hoffman," answered Nichols.

Dismounting, they tethered their horses at the hitch rail. Chamberlain looked down the street. "Looks like there's two other hotels. The Arizona and…" he squinted to read the sign three blocks away "…and the Mayflower."

"Shouldn't take long, then," said Nichols, stepping onto the board sidewalk.

The two outlaws approached the desk in the hotel lobby. A short fat man with a shiny bald head emerged from a back room.

"You gentlemen want one room or two?" he asked in a squeaky voice.

"Just some information," Chamberlain said without smiling. "You got a roomer here by the name of Hoffman? Richard Hoffman?"

"No sir."

"You sure?"

"Yes sir."

"Have you had a Richard Hoffman here in the past few days?

"No sir."

Chamberlain leaned over the desk, putting his fat ugly nose within two inches of the clerk's nose. "You haven't even checked the register, shorty, how can you be so sure?"

The clerk's eyes widened in fear. "'Cause business hasn't been that good, sir," he answered.

"There's just two other hotels in this here town. Right?" Chamberlain asked.

"Y-yes sir." The clerk swallowed hard. "Th-the Arizona and the M-Mayflower."

As the two ill-smelling outlaws turned and walked out the door, the clerk pulled a handkerchief from his hip pocket and mopped his entire head.

Leading their horses to the Arizona Hotel and tying them to the hitchrail, they entered the lobby. A short, heavy-set man with a ruddy complexion stood behind the desk. "May I help you gentlemen?" he asked.

Chamberlain smiled, showing his few unsightly teeth. "Yeah. Just need some information. You got an hombre registered here by the name of Hoffman? Richard Hoffman?"

Very businesslike, the clerk ran his finger down the open register. Flipping his finger off the bottom of the page, he said with a smile, "No sir, sure don't."

"How about within the last week?" Chamberlain asked.

Turning the page back, he tilted the register upward so Chamberlain could not see it. "No sir. No sir, sure haven't."

The ugly man jerked the register away from the stubby fingers of the clerk, whose face paled. His eyes fell on the name. "Richard Hoffman. Room five," he said in a flat monotone.

Reaching over the desk with his left hand, Chamberlain grabbed a fistful of shirt and jerked the trembling clerk hard against the desk's edge. A heavy grunt escaped the plump man's lips. Opening his right hand, he slapped and backhanded his face several times. "What did you lie to me for?" he asked.

The clerk swallowed hard, trying to find his voice. Chamberlain shoved him hard. He bounced off the wall behind the desk and slid to the floor. Spinning on his heels and heading for the stairs, Chamberlain said, "C'mon, Will."

The clerk pulled himself to his feet, breathing heavily. He could hear Chamberlain pounding on the door of room five overhead. The pounding stopped. The two men were talking. He could not distinguish their words. Again he heard the pounding.

"Got to get the sheriff," he said to himself. Slipping through the gate at the end of the desk, he started for the front door.

"Hold it!" Chamberlain barked.

Slowly, the clerk turned around to face the outlaws.

"Where you goin'?"

"No-nowhere, sir," he stammered.

"How come you lied to me about McCl— er, Hoffman?"

The clerk walked to a chair and sat down. "Please, sir," he said, "Mr. McClain isn't in town now."

"McClain? So you know who he is?" Nichols asked.

"Yes sir. Sheriff from Tucson cornered him at the Silver Spur. He's taking him to Tucson to stand trial for murder."

"You mean Matt Blake?" Chamberlain's jaw dropped.

"Yes sir. Matt Blake."

"When did all this happen?"

"Blake arrested him night before last. I think they left yesterday morning."

"You think? Whaddya mean, you think?"

The clerk adjusted himself in the chair. "They had McClain in jail. So I'm not sure exactly when they left."

"Did they take the stage?" Will Nichols queried.

"I-I don't know, sir. Please, I can't tell you anymore."

"Let's go, Will," Chamberlain said. Looking down at the ashen-faced clerk, he said, "Where's the stage office?"

"Across the street and up about half a block," the heavy man answered. "But it's probably closed now." Eyeing the clock on the lobby wall, he went on. "Sam Pitts…he's the clerk at the stage office…lives at the boarding house on the corner. J-just a couple doors from the office. It's Ma Hartley's Boarding House. You can't miss it."

When the two outlaws were gone, the clerk heaved a sigh of relief. Standing to his feet, he waddled to the desk on shaky legs. Passing through the gate, he reached under the desk and produced a half-empty whiskey bottle and a shot glass. With trembling hand, he tipped the bottle and splattered its contents on the desk. He could not steady his hand to pour the whiskey in the glass.

"Oh well," he said, and stuck the tip of the bottle in his mouth and downed it.

The sun had dropped below the horizon, setting the long slender clouds afire, when the two outlaws approached the livery stable. Sam Pitts had advised them that Sheriff Matt Blake had come to Yuma by stage, but had bought two horses from Zeke Ryle, the local hostler. He and his prisoner had not left town on the stage.

Banging on the door of the livery office, Chamberlain hollered, "Hey! Hostler!"

Pitts had informed them that Zeke Ryle had his living quarters at the stable. "Jest a minnit! Jest a minnit!" he called from inside.

The door opened a few inches. A little man with a wrinkled face stared at them. "Whut kin I do for ya?"

"We want to ask you some questions," Chamberlain said.

"Whut kind of questions?" Zeke Ryle asked with a note of irritation in his voice.

Will Nichols threw his big shoulder against the door, sending Ryle sprawling on the floor. The two men quickly stepped inside, closing the door. The combined odor of leather, hay, horses, and manure filled their nostrils. The building was dark, except for a lantern's flickering light coming from a doorway in the back.

Chamberlain helped the old man to his feet. "We ain't lookin' for trouble, mister," he said. "We just need some information."

Zeke Ryle dusted off the seat of his britches. He turned and started for the lighted room to the rear. "C'mon back and set a spell," he said, putting a friendlier tone to his voice.

The two outlaws followed Ryle into a small room equipped with a pot-bellied stove, an old chest of drawers, a crude table with one chair, and a rickety old bed. A kerosene lamp sat on the table. A dust-covered picture of Abraham Lincoln hung crooked on one wall, next to a slicker slung over a wooden peg. A rusty old shotgun stood in a corner alongside a pile of indescribable debris.

The wrinkled old man scraped the lone chair across the floor. Looking at Chamberlain with wary eyes, he said, "Set down, young feller." Motioning to the dilapidated bed, he looked at Nichols. "You kin set there."

The bed creaked under Nichols' weight. Chamberlain made no move to occupy the chair. "You take the chair, Pop," he said. "I'll stand."

Zeke Ryle lowered his thin frame onto the chair. "Whut kin I tell you boys?"

"We understand you sold a couple horses to the sheriff from Tucson," Chamberlain opened up.

"Yep. Shore did. Yestidy mornin'. Sold him a big zebra dun and a pack horse. You a friend of his'n?"

Chamberlain cleared his throat. "Not exactly."

"Shore was a mean lookin' hombre he had with him," the old man said.

"That hombre is our friend, Pop," Nichols said. "We want to know which way they were travelin' to Tucson."

"If you boys are figgerin' to overpower Matt Blake, you

might better take on a nest of rattlesnakes!" Ryle said, his voice raising to a high pitch.

"Which way did they go?" Chamberlain said with a snap. He scowled at Zeke Ryle. "Did they take the stagecoach route…or did they light out straight for Tucson?"

"I heard tell that Blake once shot it out with six gun-slingers at one time," the old man said, "six of 'em! Used one bullet for each. Killed 'em all!"

Chamberlain whipped out his revolver, pointed the gun at Ryle's nose, and said, "Which way?"

"Straight."

Chamberlain smiled. "That'd be toward Indian Head Spring, right?"

"Yessir."

"Then what?" Will Nichols asked.

"They'd go straight east another fifty, sixty miles to Tapanic Tank. Trail would take 'em from there to Diago Spring. 'Bout eighty miles. That's the last water before Tucson."

Chamberlain frowned. "Why wouldn't they follow the stage route? Wouldn't that be safer?"

"Blake figgered to stay clear of the outlaw scum that follers the stage route," said Ryle.

Nichols sprang from the bed, closing his fist to strike the old man. Rob Chamberlain grasped the younger outlaw's wrist. "Save your strength for somebody who can fight back, Will."

Chamberlain looked down at Ryle. "What time did they leave yesterday, Pop?"

"'Bout seven o'clock."

"Looks like they got a couple days on us, Will," said the ugly flat-nosed man. "We'd better plan to light outta here before sunup."

Neither man said another word to Zeke Ryle. Leaving him to his rustic surroundings, they made their way to the door of the stable and stepped out on the street. The fresh air felt good to their lungs.

Indian Head Spring was situated on an elevated mound surrounded by heaps of massive, sun-blistered rocks. Huge cracks in the earth weaved among the cacti, mesquite, and ocotillo, joining with the dead volcano cones to tell their ancient story. The earth had gone into angry convulsions, spewing lava in a bubbling flood. Amidst the thundering shower of molten rock, there had been a great upheaval of stone and dirt. When the earth's quaking had ceased and the smoke had cleared, the fractured mound issued forth a spring of water. Emerging somewhere from the mysterious depths of volcanic earth, the cool, clear water rested in this citadel of stone at the base of a giant, slender rock.

The great rock was comparatively smooth from its base upward. At the top, it seemed to burst forth as if in prophetic excellence, and formed an almost perfect shape of an Indian's head. It was as though old Mother Earth had known that one day white men would invade the Indian's land in the north and force them to take up habitation in the parched and burning desert. She would provide water and mark the place with a predominant insignia.

The Indian profile was cast in lengthening shadow as Matt Blake dismounted the zebra dun. Turning to Gray Wolf, he said, "Now you and your bucks can get a cool drink."

As the dust-enshrouded Yaquis dismounted and followed their leader up the rock-strewn mound, Matt Blake studied the wagon tracks imprinted in the dust. "Still about a day ahead of us," he said to himself. "They camped here last night."

When the last of the seven Yaquis had disappeared behind the rocks, Duke McClain slid off his bay and walked up close to the sheriff. In a half-whisper, he said, "Blake, those savages are gonna kill us! You're a fool if you can't see that! I'm your prisoner. You've gotta do somethin' to protect me!"

"I'm not concerned about Gray Wolf," Blake retorted. "He counts on me as his blood brother. It's Samanti that worries me."

"Then let's light outta here before he shows!"

"We will leave in the morning," the sheriff said. "The horses must have rest."

"Yer gonna git us tortured and murdered!" cried McClain, his eyes wild. "I'm gittin' out." The little man spun on his heels and started for his horse. As he lifted his left foot toward the stirrup, he heard the double click of Blake's .45.

Still facing the bay, McClain paused and said, "You won't shoot me, Sheriff. You want me to dance on the end of a rope too bad."

Swinging his leg over the saddle, he turned to look at Blake. The tall man's cold blue eyes seemed to look right through him. The Colt was leveled at his heart.

"You spur that horse, you're a dead man," Blake said in a cold monotone.

McClain swallowed hard. His Adam's apple slid down his throat and bobbed back in place. The sheriff's face had the appearance of solid granite. The deep lines in his brow and the crow's feet in the corners of his eyes seemed chiseled in a visage of cold marble. Blake's eyes were steady, pale, and as blue as the desert sky. They telegraphed an unmistakable message.

McClain held the reins taut. There was no question. If the horse made a false start, a .45 slug would tear through his heart.

"Get off the horse," Blake commanded.

"I'd—I'd just as soon take your bullet as to be tortured by them vicious savages," Duke said, finding his voice.

"You haven't been tortured yet. I told you, we are safe as far as Gray Wolf is concerned. Samanti isn't here yet. We're pulling out at dawn. If he shows up before we leave, we still have a chance."

Both men could hear the Indians laughing and frolicking at the spring. They were dousing each other with the cool water.

"If you spur that horse, you don't have a lick of a chance," Blake continued. "Get off the horse."

"I'll make you a deal," McClain said.

"No deals! Get off the horse!"

"Let's you and me square off. We're gonna die if Samanti shows up. At least give me a sporting chance, Sheriff. If you beat me to the draw, at least I won't have to die bein' tortured…and I'll take my chances skinnin' across the desert."

Gray Wolf and Quiet Bear had emerged from the rocks and were descending the mound together. They were soaked from head to foot. The other five were following several paces behind. Gray Wolf lifted his eyes and focused on the two white men. He gripped Quiet Bear's arm and pulled him to a stop. The others followed suit.

The Indians were within earshot. They heard Matt Blake say, "I promised you a noose, little man. I aim to keep that promise."

"You kill me now, big man, and I'll never wear that noose. They don't hang dead men. What good is a dead man's noose?"

"Get off the horse," the sheriff said through clenched teeth. "Now."

Their eyes deadlocked in an impasse. The little outlaw glared, hate boiling within him. He pulled back his lips, showed his yellow teeth, and sucked at them. Neither man blinked.

"Hey, Gray Wolf!" McClain said, without moving his eyes. "I just challenged your blood brother here to a shootout."

Gray Wolf stepped closer, followed at an angle by Quiet Bear. Both stood behind the sheriff.

"That critter standin' there holdin' a gun on me. You'd better watch out for it. Calls itself a human!" McClain chuckled deep in his throat, his eyes still deadlocked with Blake's. "It ain't no human. It's a yellow-bellied diamondback. Carries its noise in its mouth instead of its tail."

Matt Blake did not hear him coming. He only saw Gray Wolf streak past him. The bay shied and bolted, but not before the swift Indian had pulled McClain to the ground with a thud. Flattening the outlaw to the earth on his back, he pointed his right knee to McClain's belly just under the rib cage and came down hard.

McClain let out a yell. Gray Wolf repeated the action. McClain hollered again.

"I told you this morning, yellow hair," Gray Wolf said, "Matt Blake is Gray Wolf's blood brother. What you say of him, you say of me!"

Holstering his Colt, the tall man stepped forward. "Let him up."

Gray Wolf's muscles rippled and corded as he rose to his feet. With one hand, he gripped McClain's collar and yanked him to a standing position. McClain pursed his lips, turned, and walked toward the sheriff. As he approached the tall man, he spit in his face.

Gray Wolf lunged, grasped the back of McClain's collar, and snapped him to the ground. Blake shouted, "Don't hurt him, Gray Wolf!" He was wiping the spittle from his face with his sleeve.

The muscular Yaqui looked up as if to say, "He has it coming!"

Matt Blake set his jaw. He lifted McClain to his feet. Looking him square in the eye, he said, "He's got his shootout."

Breathing hard, McClain smiled, displaying his mouthful of yellow teeth. "Now you're talkin', Sheriff!"

"I'm going to untie your hands," said Blake. "I want you to get the stiffness worked out of your wrists. Gray Wolf will accompany you to the spring. Get yourself a long, cool drink." Blake eyed him heavily as he untied the rope on the outlaw's wrists.

There was something askew about the look in Blake's eyes. McClain couldn't read it. What did it mean?

Blake looked toward the sun. "There's about two hours of light left. We'll square off in one hour." The sheriff turned and began loosening the cinch on the dun's saddle.

McClain studied him for a moment, rubbing his wrists. There was something behind this change of mind toward a shootout…something besides a spit in the face.

Laying the saddle on the ground, Blake looked up at McClain. "Go on and get yourself some water."

Gray Wolf nudged him with a stiff finger. Together, they climbed the mound and disappeared behind the rocks. Quiet Bear approached the sheriff. "You really going to shoot it out with ugly man?" he asked.

"Yep."

"But white man's law. Doesn't it say he should hang?"

"Yep. He will."

"Quiet Bear not understand."

"You will. Now let's water the horses."

Bending over the spring, the little outlaw buried his face in the cool water. Drinking deeply, he gasped and gulped until his thirst was slaked. He rolled over and lay flat in the cool shade under the watchful eye of the muscular Gray Wolf. The minutes passed slowly.

Two bucks came with the oak casks and filled them, leaving as quickly as they had come.

Rubbing his wrists, McClain thought of the strange look in the sheriff's eyes. "Can't figger it," he said to Gray Wolf.

"Can't figure what?" the Indian asked.

"Why the lawman suddenly gave in to a shootout."

"You spit in his face," Gray Wolf said. "Mighty big insult."

"Naw. That's not it. He's got somethin' up his sleeve. He knows I can beat him. I'm fast, Injun. Mighty fast! He's gonna pull somethin' dirty. He won't face me fair and square!"

"You are wrong, yellow hair. Matt Blake is good man. He will not play dirty."

A long, tall figure suddenly appeared, looming over the lounging outlaw. "You worried, sonny?"

"I want my own gun, Blake! I want to load it myself!" exclaimed McClain, leaping to his feet.

Gray Wolf snapped to attention, eyeing the little man with the beak nose.

"You'll get it just like you want it," replied Blake, as he knelt down and dipped his face in the spring. After a long drink, he stood up. Letting the refreshing substance drip from his stubbled face, he looked toward the sky. The lowering sun could not be seen from inside the rock citadel.

With his sleeve, the tall man wiped the water from his graying moustache and said, "You got about a half-hour, McClain." Motioning to Gray Wolf, he said, "I want to talk to you and the bucks together."

McClain's eyes filled with a mixture of fear and fury. "Oh no you don't, Blake! You're not talkin' to those savages without me!"

Blake's eyes snapped in unison with his mouth. "You're going to get a fair shake, 'Mad-dog.' That's more than you gave Margie Kendall…and probably a hundred others."

The sheriff saw the fire in the outlaw's eyes. Turning about-face, he stepped toward the opening in the rocks. "Let's go," he said.

As the trio descended the mound, Matt Blake said, "Duke, you gather some mesquite for our campfire. That'll help loosen your hands."

Fury flooded the outlaw's face. "I may be your prisoner, big man, but I ain't your servant! You just have one of these redskin swine do your dirty work!"

Gray Wolf threw his feet into McClain's legs, tripping him. The two men rolled down the mound, raising a cloud of dust. When the dust cleared, the Yaqui was on top of the outlaw, holding the point of his knife on the protruding Adam's apple. His eyes bulging from their sockets, McClain cried, "Get him off me, Blake! Get him off me!"

The sheriff said nothing. Gray Wolf pressed the knife tight against the skin.

"Blake!" he screamed. "He's gonna kill me!"

Silence prevailed.

Sweat was pouring from McClain's face. His breathing was uneven. He ran his tongue over his lips. "Blake! Do something!"

Gray Wolf spoke through clenched teeth. "You apologize for smart talk to Gray Wolf's blood brother."

"I'm sorry, Blake! I'm sorry!" screamed McClain, expecting to feel the knife blade released.

"Now you apologize to Yaqui braves for calling us swine!"

"I'm sorry!" the frightened man blurted out.

"For what?" asked Gray Wolf.

"For calling you swine!" The knife remained against his throat.

"Now you tell Sheriff Matt Blake you would be happy to do a swine's work because you are a swine."

"I would be happy to do a swine's work because I am a swine," McClain said.

"Louder, swine," Gray Wolf commanded. "Louder!"

McClain gasped for breath. "I WOULD BE HAPPY TO DO A SWINE'S WORK BECAUSE I AM A SWINE!" he shouted.

Bounding to his feet, Gray Wolf sheathed his knife. "Go gather wood for the fire, swine."

Slowly, the wiry outlaw rose to his feet, rubbing his Adam's apple. "Better get with it, Duke," Blake said, "you've only got a few minutes."

Without a word, McClain moved out among the mesquite, gathering branches. The sheriff turned to Gray Wolf. "How long will you wait for Samanti?"

"We will stay here until he comes," replied the Yaqui. "You no doubt have noticed game tracks. We should have food. We have plenty of water." Gray Wolf paused for a long moment. "My brother…my brother, I wish to tell you that…that…"

"Tell me what?" ejaculated Blake.

"Yaquis are not going to ride with Samanti."

"Why not?" asked the tall man.

"Since you saved our lives, we no longer carry terrible hatred for white eyes. We discussed it at spring awhile ago. We agreed to stay and meet Samanti. We will explain our feelings and go back to Yaqui reservation."

"Samanti may not take that too good," Blake said.

"We discussed that, too. Our leader, Yellow Fang, made promise to meet Samanti here. We will honor that promise. Samanti is Gray Wolf's friend. He will understand."

"I hope so," said Blake.

"It is best if you leave before Samanti arrives," Gray Wolf said with caution. "I must send up smoke signal tomorrow morning. We will bury yellow hair for you."

"You have confidence I will outdraw McClain?"

"There is no doubt in Gray Wolf's heart."

The firewood was piled high. Duke McClain dusted off his hands. The cockiness having returned to full force, he approached Matt Blake. "Sun's goin' down, Sheriff. Ready to square off?"

"Yep," replied Blake without a trace of emotion. "My saddle is right over there. Go get your gun. Quiet Bear will cover you with the repeater while you load up and practice a draw or two. Wouldn't want you to get overconfident with that gun in your hand."

The little outlaw ran and fell on his knees beside Blake's saddle. Fumbling with the buckle, he produced his revolver. Still wearing his holster and gun belt, he quickly began thumbing bullets into the chamber. Snapping it expertly, he spun the cylinder. Dropping it into the holster, he drew it with a flash. He repeated the draw several times. Quiet Bear eyed him cautiously.

Walking briskly to where the sheriff stood with Gray Wolf, he said, "You gonna make these Indians give their word that after I gun you down, they'll let me ride outta here unmolested?"

"You heard him," Blake said, turning to Gray Wolf.

The Yaqui worked his jaw. The other six braves were standing near, listening. "You have my word, yellow hair."

McClain narrowed his eyes. "You ain't rigged a trap for me, have ya, Sheriff?"

"Nope," Blake replied. "If you gun me down, you can ride away."

"All right," McClain said with arrogance, "let's go after it!"

Both men stepped away from the horses, several paces. Quiet Bear still held his rifle ready. McClain backed up until the two men were about forty feet apart.

Matt Blake stood spread-legged with a slight droop to his shoulders. His open right hand hung just above the butt of his Colt .45.

Grinning widely, with a strange, insane look in his eyes, Duke McClain gave a vivid appearance of a mad dog about to close in for the kill. His steady hand hovered over the .44. His feet were spread apart. There was a slight buckle in his knees.

The tall sheriff studied the eyes of the outlaw. He had found by experience that a man will signal with his eyes before his hand drops for the gun.

A hushed repression hovered in the cooling desert air. The Yaqui beheld the scene with bated breath. Time seemed to stand still.

Matt Blake concentrated on the narrow-set beady eyes of the heartless killer. He thought of the forty-six other men who had challenged his speed in moments identical to this.

Suddenly, McClain's eyes flashed the signal.

CHAPTER SIX

amanti's two scouts hunkered down in a shallow gully, watching the seven Indians and two white men moving about the base of the tall, slender rock. Soon the Yaquis climbed the mound and passed from sight behind the rocks.

The Apache scouts were out of earshot, but from what they saw they could tell that there was a dispute between the two white men. Suddenly the small one was in his saddle. The tall man was pointing his revolver at the mounted man.

As the argument continued, the Yaquis reappeared. All of a sudden one young buck was dragging the small man from the saddle. The Indian held the white man on the ground. Twice the scouts heard the man yell.

In a few moments the small white man was on his feet climbing toward the spring, accompanied by the buck who had downed him.

"Let us go," said one scout to the other. Bending low, they scurried behind a cluster of rocks, where they mounted horses and galloped away.

Samanti lifted up his finely chiseled face as the scouts came at full gallop. Scattering dust as they reined to a halt, they informed their leader as to the scene at Indian Head

Spring. Goading their horses with their heels, the band continued their normal pace.

"You saw only seven Yaquis?" queried Samanti, frowning.

"Yes. Seven," answered the scout at his right.

"Could there be more among the rocks?" asked Samanti, revealing a tone of disappointment.

"Not enough horses for more," the scout riding his left replied.

Samanti's brain was reeling. What could have happened? Was Yellow Fang or Gray Wolf among them? His scouts had never laid eyes on either. They would not know. Who were the white men? According to the scouts' report, neither whites nor Indians were holding each other prisoners.

Thoughts raced through his mind. If the Yaquis were not bound, why hadn't they killed the hated white men? Certainly Yellow Fang and Gray Wolf must be dead. Neither of them would let White Eyes live any longer than it would take to kill them.

Samanti spoke again. "Did the Yaquis have rifles?"

"We did not see any rifles," answered the scout on the left. "Of course, that does not mean they do not have them."

Samanti wondered if they would have ammunition. He had counted on that. He thought of the heavily armed cavalry which was not far behind. The Apaches had skirted a couple of miles to the east of the normal trail. Staying ahead by at least three hours, they would elude the army scouts and leave no signs as to their whereabouts. Samanti would need ammunition to ambush the army platoon at Indian Head Spring.

Just ahead of the Apache band was a gradual rise. The mesquite, cacti, and ocotillo were thickening about them. The worried leader turned his leathered face toward the west. He could see the last flames of the sun on the horizon. It would be dark in less than an hour.

Samanti was pondering on the method of approach he would make at the spring. Deep in thought, he did not notice it at first. By the time he had crested the rise, it caught his eye. The sun's last pink rays were highlighting the Indian head at the pinnacle of the tall, slender rock.

A warm flow of pride came over him. There was something awesome and majestic about the jagged facial features. The young Apache was proud to be an Indian.

The roar of a gun clattered through the desert air. Samanti raised his right hand as he spun the Appaloosa around.

"Quick! Back over the rise!"

In a cloud of dust, the Apaches retreated below the crest of the rise and dismounted. Bending low, Samanti called for Hondo to follow him, while he motioned for the others to wait where they stood.

Moments later, the two Apaches were bellied down on the low side of the crest.

"It's getting too dark to see that far," said Hondo.

"It sounded like a pistol," said Samanti, "but we are even too far for a rifle."

"Maybe they just try to warn us," Hondo said.

"We now must wait until morning. Something is wrong, Hondo. We will make approach with sunrise."

Quickly Samanti and his lieutenant made their way back

to the restless band. "We will make camp here," said Samanti. "We have water for tonight. Go to spring at sunrise."

In the split second between the time Duke McClain's eyes unwittingly flashed the signal and his hand dropped to his gun, Blake's blurred hand cleared leather and the Colt .45 roared. McClain's hat flew from his head. His gun was only halfway out of the holster.

Holding it in that position, he looked down the smoking barrel of the tall man's .45. Awe-struck for the moment, McClain's lips went white to match his pallid face.

"Who you been drawing against," Blake asked, "ninety-year-old cripples?" His voice was cold as a mountain wind in January. "I could have taken a nap while you were finding your gun. I figured you were just a lot of talk."

The outlaw's narrow-set eyes were bulging. They did not blink until Matt Blake stepped forward and pulled the .44 from its holster, releasing it from McClain's numb fingers. Breaking it open, he spun the cylinder, dropping the six cartridges in the dust. McClain still had not moved.

Gray Wolf smiled. "'Mad-dog' looks more like whipped puppy!"

Towering over the outlaw, who now seemed even smaller, the sheriff said, "You and I are going to bathe and shave."

Losing the sun in the western sand, the desert began to cool. A soft breeze was stirring the mesquite leaves as somewhere far out over the sand a quail called to its mate.

Amid the rocks at the pool, Quiet Bear held a rough-

hewn torch as Matt Blake poured water over the naked lathered body of Duke McClain.

"Scrub hard, Duke," said Blake, "this soap will make you
smell better."

Duke McClain was shivering and scrubbing as the cool
night wind whipped around the rocks. Blake took note of all
the black-and-blue marks the slender little outlaw had sus-
tained.

After bathing and shaving by torchlight, the two white
men sat around the fire and ate supper with the Yaquis. Duke
McClain had said nothing since his hat was removed by the
sheriff's bullet. Shoveling beans past his yellow teeth, he
smacked his lips and gulped like a hungry dog.

Holding his tin coffee cup in both hands, the Tucson lawman studied McClain, who never raised his eyes. His pride
was injured and his ego had suffered a heavy blow.

Finishing his meal, McClain rolled a cigarette and sat in
silence, blowing smoke toward the stars. He avoided eye con-
tact with Blake.

The sheriff and Gray Wolf walked together out into the
darkness. "It is best if you leave by sunrise, white brother," the
thick-chested Indian said with concern. "I think Samanti
would honor my feelings toward you, but I do not know his
frame of mind."

"We will go at sunup," Blake said.

Gray Wolf cleared his throat. "Matt Blake."

"Yes, red brother?"

"Were you really sure you could outdraw yellow hair?"

"Yep."

"How could you know?"

"It can't be explained. You just feel it."

"You never intended to kill him?"

"Nope. He's going to hang. I promised him a noose. I aim to keep my promise."

"You never met a man as fast as you, huh?"

"If I had, Gray Wolf, would I be standing here?"

Gray Wolf chuckled. "Indian sometimes ask dumb questions."

Slowly the duo returned to the fire. The Indians sat on one side of the fire, McClain on the other. "Time to turn in, Duke," Blake said. "We're pulling out at sunup."

"We will have a man on watch all night, white brother," Gray Wolf said. "You get a good night's sleep for journey tomorrow."

The tall man smiled, placing his right hand on the Yaqui's muscular shoulder. "Thank you, red brother."

Matt Blake had placed McClain's saddle beside his own. "Time to lace up your wrists, Duke," he said as they approached the saddles.

McClain spoke his first words since his humiliation at sundown. "Aw, please, Sheriff. I ain't gonna pull nuthin'!"

"As far as I know," retorted Blake, "it hasn't snowed in Panama yet…and this sure isn't Tucson." Lifting the rope from his saddle horn, he said, "Put your hands together."

McClain got a pitiful look on his face and looked up at Blake with wincing eyes. Blake thought how much he looked like a seven-year-old boy. Then he thought again that nobody could get that ugly in seven years.

The outlaw's voice was squeaky. "Please, Sheriff. Please."

Blake said, "All right. You go tell Gray Wolf that he should tell his bucks that if you so much as lift your head during the night, they are to put bullets in both your legs."

McClain swallowed hard, sending his protruding Adam's apple on another journey. Cautiously he walked to Gray Wolf. The Indian had already heard the conversation, but he let McClain say the whole thing, just for the sheer pleasure of it.

"Whatever yellow hair say," replied Gray Wolf, with a sparkle in his dark eyes, "we would be most pleased to shoot you!"

The outlaw walked back to his saddle, sat down on the ground, and slipped off his boots. Pulling the blanket over his body, he pillowed his head on the saddle.

It was another moonless night. As the fire dwindled, the stars overhead seemed to grow brighter. The young buck on watch stirred the fire, putting on some more wood. Duke McClain noticed the Indian eyeing him. They knew how the yellow-haired outlaw hated them. Any one of them would find great pleasure in shooting him.

McClain listened for Blake's steady breathing. It was not noticeable.

"Blake!" he whispered loudly.

"Yep."

"You knew all along you could outdraw me!"

"Yep."

"You hadn't planned to kill me, had you?"

"Nope."

"What would you have done if I'da pulled my gun after you shot my hat off?"

"I'd have smashed your gun arm."

"What if you'd missed?"

"Never have."

"You mean you have winged a lot of men instead of killin' 'em?" McClain asked with surprise.

"Yep. Only took 'em out when I had to."

"How come?"

"Rather see 'em hang."

The outlaw offered no more questions. All was silent. McClain had seen many a moonless night, but this was the ugliest, blackest night of his life. His confidence of escape had received a staggering blow. He thought of Chamberlain and Nichols. Where had they been? Why had they not shown up in Yuma? Maybe a posse had shot them down.

McClain had planned to rob the payroll of a mining company that was working just outside of Yuma. It was brought in on the stagecoach once a month from Phoenix. It was not a job he could tackle by himself. When the payroll came in, Chamberlain and Nichols were already two days late. McClain had to watch helplessly as the money was unloaded from the stage and carted off to the mine.

The Yaquis drew his attention as they changed the guard and built up the fire. Sleep seemed an elusive thing. Closing his eyes, he tried to relax. Matt Blake was breathing evenly now.

McClain thought of what lay ahead in Tucson. He shook his head, trying to cast off such thoughts. He raised his head to turn over. The Yaqui guard jumped to his feet, leveling Talking Rifle's Winchester repeater at the outlaw.

"Sorry," he said. "Havin' trouble gettin' to sleep." He remembered hearing the sheriff say that the Winchester still had four cartridges in the magazine.

Settling down again, thoughts of Tucson jumped back into his brain. They had not disturbed his sleep the night before. He had clung to the hope of provoking the sheriff into gunplay and walking away the victor. That hope had forever passed into oblivion. He had never seen a man so fast.

He thought about the determined lawman's promise. A wild beast called to its mate somewhere out in the desert. Slowly, the heavy shades of slumber overwhelmed his thoughts. The distant beast called again. Duke McClain did not hear it.

Many people do their heaviest dreaming within two hours before awakening. So it was with the outlaw. The Yaqui guard just noticed the slight hint of gray on the eastern horizon when he heard McClain groaning in his sleep. He turned to look. In the dim light of the final glowing embers from the fire, he could see McClain tossing his head to-and-fro.

In his dreams, McClain was walking toward the gallows at dawn. He could see the crude wooden structure towering toward the sky. He could feel the soft morning breeze on his face. Stiffening his wobbly legs he tried to stop his forward movement. His heels dug in the dirt, but it was to no avail. Something…someone stronger than himself was forcing him toward the gallows.

He tried to call out, but his voice refused. He could feel

the sweat running into his eyes. Raising his arm, he brushed away the stinging moisture. He blinked several times, trying to clear his vision. Looking upward as he approached the gallows he saw a crowd of people standing around the crude structure. At first their faces were blurred. Then, one by one they came into focus. These were his victims. Men, women, and children he had murdered in cold blood. Each one had a hand cupped upward, beckoning with the index finger.

Their eyes! He tried to scream. They had no eyes! The sockets were just white pools, empty white pools. He scanned the crowd as he approached them. There were ranchers and their families, the bank employees, and people he had shot down in the streets. There was Margie Kendall, sightless white pools where her eyes should be. She was screaming at him, "Murderer! Murderer! Murderer!"

A strong man behind him was pushing him up the steps. He tried to see who it was, but something kept him from turning around. Midway up the creaking steps, he paused to look down. Now the crowd was pointing at him and laughing. Oh, those horrible white pools! From the elevated position, he recognized the young rancher's wife he had shot down in Burlington. He had shot her, he remembered, from his horse…at just about this angle. As he took another step, he tried to find her husband's face in the crowd.

The strong arm at his back hurried him upward. As he reached the platform, he looked down at the trap door. The laughter of the crowd thundered in his ears.

He was forced to step on the trap door and then violently spun around. He was looking into Matt Blake's face. Blake's eyes were normal. He hadn't died! The sheriff began to laugh with the crowd.

Something brushed his head. Lifting his eyes, he saw the noose swaying in the breeze. Again, he tried to scream. Nothing. The sheriff had a piece of black cloth in his hand. "I promised you this noose, McClain," he said in a half-whisper, "and I keep my promises."

As the hood dropped over his head, everything went black. Suddenly there was a loud noise, like a sharp clap of thunder…

Duke McClain awoke with a sudden start and sat up, his eyes wide. By the light of early dawn, he could see Quiet Bear standing a few feet away, holding the familiar rifle. Blue smoke was sifting from the muzzle.

The rest of the camp was on its feet now. "Sorry to awaken you like this," Quiet Bear said, "but I had to shoot now, or miss the chance."

Scrambling to his feet, Duke McClain joined the cluster of men. They were watching a small herd of antelope bounding northward, about a quarter of a mile away. About a hundred yards out, one antelope lay motionless on the ground.

Gray Wolf spoke a command in Apache to four bucks, who ran out to retrieve the fallen antelope.

"They stray up here from Mexico," said Matt Blake. "No doubt smelled the water."

"You can have antelope steak for breakfast, my brother," said Gray Wolf.

"Afraid we won't have time, red brother," replied Blake. "Jerky will have to be our meat. Yellow hair and I must be going. Sun will be up in half an hour."

The Yaquis filled one oak cask with fresh water and mounted it on the gray, balancing it with sacks of grain. Downing breakfast quickly, the two white men saddled their horses.

Matt Blake removed the familiar piece of short rope from the saddle horn. "Here you go, Duke," he said. The wiry outlaw knew it was useless to argue. Facing the tall sheriff, he extended his coupled wrists.

"Matt Blake!"

It was Gray Wolf's voice. Turning in response, Blake's eyes widened. One of the horses nickered. The nicker was returned by Samanti's Appaloosa. There they were, mounted in a semicircle. Fifty-nine Apaches, their skin appearing as blistered sanguine in the light of the sunrise.

Samanti, tall and erect on his mount, bore a silent dignity. Fifty-seven remained in the semicircle some fifty yards from the campsite. Samanti was riding slowly forward with Hondo just to the rear of his left flank.

Each Apache held his rifle in plain view. It was only a bluff. There was not one bullet among them.

His hands still free, Duke McClain bolted for Quiet Bear, snatched the Winchester, cocked it, and raised it to his shoulder. At the same time, he was screaming like a madman, cursing the Apaches with the vilest of language.

Aiming at Samanti, he pulled the trigger. A split second before the gun barked, Gray Wolf tackled him full force, sending the bullet into the ground. The muscular Yaqui picked up McClain and smashed him in the face with a right cross. McClain went down like a rag doll.

At the same instant the deranged outlaw had raised the rifle, Samanti and Hondo reined in, but the band of Apaches behind them goaded their horses to charge. Coming at full gallop, they began pulling their knives.

Matt Blake whipped his .45 from its holster. The Apaches were whooping as they charged.

Gray Wolf, leaping over the unconscious outlaw, ran toward the oncoming charge. Waving his arms frantically, he cried for them to stop. As the thundering band drew abreast of their leader, he raised his hand. In a cloud of dust, they brought their horses to an abrupt half.

"Samanti!" cried the Yaqui leader. "It's me! Gray Wolf!"

Turning to his warriors, who were now less than twenty yards from Blake and the Yaquis, Samanti spoke in Apache, commanding them to remain where they were. As Matt Blake holstered his Colt, he watched Samanti dismount the Appaloosa in one smooth motion and shake hands Indian style with Gray Wolf. It was noticeable that even with the warm greeting to his long-time friend, Samanti was not smiling.

"Yellow Fang?" asked Samanti, looking past Gray Wolf toward the campsite.

"Dead. Cavalry." Swinging his arm toward his braves, he said, "This is all that is left."

Samanti wanted to ask about ammunition. He dared not. Looking at the revolver in Matt Blake's holster, he said, "These white men not your prisoners?"

Gray Wolf explained that the tall man who wore the star

was the sheriff from Tucson. The man on the ground who was beginning to stir was the sheriff's prisoner. A low moan came from the bleeding mouth of Duke McClain.

A deep scowl marred the handsome angular face of the Apache leader. "White men must die!" Samanti cried with anger.

"No!" retorted Gray Wolf.

The Apaches sheathed their knives and once again held their rifles in a ready position.

Gray Wolf spoke quickly. "The sheriff saved our lives," he said with an indignant tone. "We were dying of thirst. He shared his water and his food with us."

Samanti's finely chiseled face remained expressionless as the two red men stood face-to-face, less than three feet apart.

"Sheriff Matt Blake is blood brother!" Gray Wolf said with feeling.

Samanti glanced over Gray Wolf's shoulder to Duke McClain, who was now trying to find his feet. Just behind him was the tall man with silver tips in his dark hair.

"Him die!" barked Samanti, pointing to McClain.

"Yes, Samanti!" shouted Hondo from behind, his voice raising to a high pitch. "Yellow-hair white man die!"

Matt Blake took hold of the staggering outlaw, who was unaware of what was transpiring at the moment. He swung him in a circular motion, setting him down where he himself had been standing.

Pulling himself to an erect position, he stood in front of McClain, he legs spread in an action pose. "Tell him no, Gray Wolf! This man is my prisoner! He must be returned to

Tucson to be punished by white man's law!"

"He tried to kill Samanti!" The Apache leader shouted, putting his thumb to his bronzed chest. The Apaches began to shout angrily, calling for McClain to die.

The outlaw had recovered sufficiently to grasp what was being said. "Don't let 'em have me, Sheriff! Don't let 'em have me!"

"Shut up!" Blake barked, without taking his eyes off Samanti.

Amidst the din, as the Apaches shouted, Samanti felt the heat of the sun on his back. He was suddenly aware that time was of the essence. They were out of ammunition and nearly out of water. The heavily armed platoon of soldiers was not far away now. They must replenish their water supply and vacate the area quickly. Although they outnumbered the soldiers, there was no way they could hold the spring with only knives. He must gain control of the spring now.

Looking over Gray Wolf's shoulder at Matt Blake, and then looking into the handsome Yaqui's dark eyes, he said, "Gray Wolf, we are long friends. You must not stand in the way. We will take yellow-hair white man and water. Then we go."

The shouting died out. The Apache bucks were straining to hear the conversation between the two leaders.

Gray Wolf wondered why Samanti seemed so anxious to leave the spring. It was apparent the Apache leader had already ascertained that the two of them would not be riding and plundering together as they had planned long ago.

"No. I cannot let you take Sheriff Blake's prisoner," Gray

Wolf said in a fixed monotone, meeting Samanti's glare head-on. "White lawman is Gray Wolf's blood brother. I ask you. Take water and go." Samanti's eyes seemed to burst into flame. Turning his head, he barked a command in Apache. Fifty-eight rifles were shouldered and aimed at the little band of Yaquis and the two white men.

Matt Blake's right hand started to move toward the butt of his .45.

CHAPTER SEVEN

The two scouts were galloping toward Sergeant Jed Cooley at full speed. Reining in, they brought their horses to a stop, lifting a cloud of dust.

"Sarge!" cried Smith. "There's some kind of a powwow goin' on at the spring!"

"Yeah!" chimed in Palmer. "Samanti and his bunch are having a verbal confrontation with some other Indians. Sarge, it looks like there's a white man or two with 'em."

"Tempers are flarin', Sarge," added Smith. "Just as we were getting into position to get a good look-see, somebody fired a rifle. The Apaches started to close in, but didn't fire a shot! They were pullin' their knives!"

The big redheaded sergeant released a smile that spread from earlobe to earlobe. "Knives, huh? How many in the bunch Samanti's facing?" He wanted to spit. His tongue felt dirty with that name on it.

"Looks like six or seven," answered Palmer.

"The old jackal would have gunned 'em down if he had picked up some ammunition!" he said. "They didn't use the knives? You said verbal confrontation?"

"Yeah, Sarge," answered Palmer. "They're havin' a toe-to-toe argument. We couldn't get close enough to hear any of it, but from the looks of things, it's gonna bust into a fight!"

"I figure that the little bunch holed up at the well must have guns, but they don't know Samanti and his bunch are out of ammunition. Samanti's not wantin' to square off with knives against those guns," said Smith.

"Heeeeee hawwwww!" shouted Cooley. "Let's go, men! I'll get my hands on that dirty redskin now!"

Pressing their horses into a full gallop, Sergeant Cooley and his eighteen men made their way toward Indian Head Spring.

Matt Blake checked his right hand. He had started to draw by impulse. "Suicide," he said to himself.

While his men leveled their empty rifles, Samanti carried through with his bluff. Out of the corner of his eye, he saw the Winchester repeater in Quiet Bears' hand. He ordered the Yaqui to give him the rifle.

Quiet Bear wanted to refuse. He thought about ejecting the remaining two cartridges, but after eyeing the fifty-eight rifles, decided against it. Reluctantly, he stepped toward Samanti and handed him the rifle.

Samanti dropped the level just enough to see that there was a cartridge in the chamber. It felt good to hold a loaded gun again. Backing up several steps until he stood just in front of Hondo's pinto, the Apache leader said to Gray Wolf, "Gray Wolf is no longer Indian! He now has heart of white man. I spare you only because of what we were together in the past."

The six Yaquis stood poised for whatever was coming next. Quiet Bear now had only his knife. The other five had rifles within reach, but only a few shells in each. They would go down in a hail of gunfire if it became necessary, but they would dive for their guns and fight to the finish.

Gray Wolf stood in a straight line between Samanti and Matt Blake. "Step out of the way," Samanti said to Gray Wolf. The Yaqui was working his jaw until the jawbones seemed to swell. His hands, hanging straight down, were working nervously, opening and closing. The muscles in his back and shoulders rippled like a field of tall grass in the wind. He did not move.

Samanti took several steps to the right, pointing the rifle at the sheriff. Blake knew he could draw and fire before Samanti could pull the trigger. If he had to die, he would take the heartless savage with him.

Gray Wolf had not moved. He watched the Apache with narrowed eyes.

"Drop your gunbelt!" Samanti barked at Blake.

Duke McClain still sat on the ground behind the tall figure of the Tucson lawman. "Blake! Do something!" he cried, half muttering with fear.

Every eye was fastened on Samanti. No one saw the nineteen blue uniforms closing in from behind the Apaches at about three hundred yards. They had split into three groups. Six were coming in from the left flank, six from the right, and seven straight up the middle. They walked their horses slowly, quietly, ready to charge at a gallop as soon as they were discovered.

Sergeant Cooley had given them strict orders to kill as many Apaches as they could. They were not to shoot the Indians with the white men. They were definitely not to shoot Samanti. The redheaded sergeant wanted him for himself. As they closed in, Cooley could feel the fingers of vengeance moving up and down his spine like little prickly needles.

The Apaches would only be able to scatter three ways. The spring at Blake's back was enclosed by giant boulders. It had no outlet. The Apaches could go right, left, or straight behind them.

Matt Blake could not see the platoon coming because of the band of mounted Apaches. Samanti was repeating his command. "Drop your gunbelt, white eyes!"

The sheriff knew that if he gunned down Samanti, they would all die. There was the possibility they would anyway. Maybe Samanti was just trying to remove the risk of Blake's fast draw. Or maybe by ordering the gunbelt dropped, he planned to let them live. At least all but McClain.

"I'll drop the gunbelt if you promise to ride out of here and leave us, without any killing," said Blake with a tone that left no question about his intention.

"We will go," retorted Samanti, "but we take yellow-hair white eyes with us."

Blake's blue eyes grew cold as ice. "No. This man has broken white man's laws. He must be punished by white man."

Duke McClain was whimpering…about to break into a full-scale cry.

Samanti shouted as he squeezed the trigger, "Then you die, too!"

Gray Wolf saw the move coming in Samanti's eyes, a fraction of a second before Blake did. Leaping in front of the muzzle, Gray Wolf took the bullet in his chest. He did not go down. He lunged for Samanti.

Blake's revolver was in his hand like a flash, but Gray Wolf was in the line of fire. Samanti cocked the rifle and fired again as Gray Wolf hit him with his body straight on. The two Indians sprawled in the dust, just as Cooley and his men opened fire.

Apaches were dropping like mallards in a duckshoot. Horses were bolting, stepping on the men on the ground. Dust and gunsmoke filled the air. Men were screaming. Horses were neighing.

One of the fallen Apache's horses bolted toward Matt Blake, leaping over two Indian leaders on the ground. The sheriff, dodging the charging horse, fell backward over Duke McClain. Springing to his feet, Blake saw Gray Wolf on the ground. Samanti was gone.

In an instant, Blake was at his side. There were two bullet holes in his chest. One to the far right, the other almost dead center. He was still breathing. Blake picked him up in his arms, carrying him as a man would hold a child. Without looking behind him, he ran up the mound into the rock enclosure. Gently placing the dying Indian on the ground next to the spring, he cupped water in his hands, dropping it into his face.

Gray Wolf opened his eyes. They were glassy, but they focused on Matt Blake's face. He coughed, spewing blood from the corners of his mouth.

Matt Blake's eyes were swimming in tears. "You saved my life, Gray Wolf!" he said, sobbing.

Gray Wolf painfully lifted his right hand, placing it on Blake's shoulder. He coughed again. Another flow of blood gushed from his mouth. He swallowed hard. A faint smile crossed his pallid lips as he squeezed Blake's shoulder.

"Matt Blake…blood brother."

He coughed a third time as his hand fell limp to the ground. His eyes closed in the sleep of death.

Samanti fought his way through the smoke and dust, still clutching the Winchester. Sinking his fingers into the mane of a frightened pinto which had lost its rider, he swung onto its back. Goading the horse with his heels, he pointed its head toward the open desert.

Corporal Alex Todd raised his rifle, but as he aimed, he recognized Samanti. Turning his horse in a circle, he saw Cooley shooting at an Apache who was riding for open space. The rifle barked in Cooley's hands. The Apache screamed as he hit the earth with a thud.

"Sarge!" shouted Todd.

Cooley spun toward him, looking through dust and smoke.

Todd pointed to the fleeing Indian. "Samanti!"

Sergeant Cooley gouged his horse, sending him into a full gallop. Samanti looked back and saw him coming. Cocking the rifle, he pointed it in Cooley's direction and pulled the trigger. The firing pin slammed down on an empty chamber. He cocked it and repeated the effort with the same result. He was keenly aware that the gaining soldiers knew he was out of bullets.

The few Apaches who had not been shot down had bolted for freedom and disappeared, scattering in every direction. The platoon, unscathed, was now following Cooley at full gallop.

Sergeant Jed Cooley's big bay gelding, chosen for speed and stamina, was gaining on the pinto pony. The pinto was having trouble dodging the giant saguaros as they thickened. Squatty clusters of Arizona cacti were scattered thickly on the desert floor.

Just as both horses reached an open spot, the big man left his saddle with his hands on the Apache. Bones crunched as they hit the earth. Cooley's horse ran a few yards and stopped beside a saguaro cactus. The pinto kept running.

Samanti scrambled to his feet, breathing hard. The sergeant stood facing him. Eighteen men pulled their horses to a stop, raising a cloud of dust.

The Apache yanked his knife from its scabbard. His eyes were wild. He pulled his lips back from his teeth like a vicious wolf about to attack.

Having lost his hat when he and Samanti hit the ground, the big man ran his fingers through his red hair and then unbuckled his gunbelt. Dropping the gunbelt to the ground, he charged the wild-eyed Apache. In a full arc, Samanti swung the knife viciously. Cooley felt the blade rip through the front of his half-buttoned shirt, but there was no pain.

The Indian lunged again with lightening speed. The knife cut only hot desert air. A massive fist caught Samanti square in the mouth. His knees buckled as he went down, spitting teeth. As he rolled over, shaking his head and trying to get up, he caught a big boot in the stomach. He rolled to his knees, his head on the ground, gasping for breath.

"Kill 'em, Sarge!" shouted one of the men.

Cooley turned and said, "Not yet. He's gonna suffer a little before I break his neck." Just as he turned back, the knife was in a flashing arc. Cooley felt something burn across his ribs. It felt like a red-hot iron. Samanti was swinging again. The big redhead grasped the wrist of the knife-hand, taking hold of the elbow with his other hand. With brute strength, he wrenched the arm. The Apache cried out in pain as the knife dropped in the dust. Gathering blood and saliva in his mouth, he spit in Cooley's face.

Still holding the arm, Cooley brought up his leg. At the same time, he brought down the arm with full force. Samanti screamed as bones cracked.

Jed Cooley thought of the avalanche back in the canyon. He lifted his leg and slammed the arm down again, shouting. "This is for Thompson, Wallace, and Runyon!" The bone popped through the skin with a loud crack. Samanti's face blanched as he screamed again, falling to the ground.

The big sergeant towered over him. The soldiers were cheering from the backs of their horses. "Kill the skunk!" one of them shouted.

The Apache was rolling in the dust in agony, vomiting. He stretched out face down and lay still, unconscious.

"Gimme your canteen, Todd," Cooley commanded. Todd lifted the strap over the saddle horn and tossed the canteen to the big man. Cooley flipped the Indian over with his foot.

Holding the canteen high, he slowly dropped the water on Semanti's swollen face.

As the Apache came to, his eyes focused on the big man standing spread-eagle over him. Letting out a wild yell to stimulate his adrenaline, he kicked Cooley in the groin. The big man doubled over in pain, noticing for the first time that his shirt was soaked with blood.

Samanti was crawling toward his knife. Cooley ran and met him at the spot. Just as the Indian reached for the knife, the sergeant kicked it away. Bending over, he picked up the Apache and lifted him over his head. While the injured red man cried out in pain, Cooley walked a few yards to a large patch of squat cactus. The needles were glistening in the desert sun.

"This is for Leonard Jenkins!" Cooley slammed him down hard on the cactus. The platoon went wild, cheering for the sergeant.

Samanti was screaming, trying to climb out of the prickly mass. Jed Cooley, bent slightly forward, stood watching. The Indian finally rolled clear of the cactus patch. His body was covered with needles, and was smarting and bleeding. He raised up on one knee, paused for a moment, and keeled over.

"Gimme that canteen again!" Cooley barked to Alex Todd. The corporal had already dismounted and retrieved the fallen canteen. He darted to Cooley, uncapped it, and placed it in his hand. Slowly he retreated to stand by his horse.

When Samanti had once again regained consciousness, the big sergeant walked back to Todd and handed him the canteen. The men were quiet.

"Now I'm gonna break his neck," Cooley said.

He turned, wincing at the pain that ran like fire over his ribs. Samanti was still on the ground. Approaching the fallen Apache, Cooley kicked off the cactus needles around the shoulders. Bending over, he put his knee behind the neck. With his right arm, he reached under the jaw, putting the neck in the crook. Samanti released a death cry. Cooley pressed his knee forward and jerked back his arm. The blood-curdling crack made Alex Todd's knees buckle. One of the soldiers let out a moan, turned his horse, and rode away, giving up his breakfast. Two more followed suit.

"Remind me to stay on Cooley's good side," Private Smith said to whomever was listening.

Several buzzards were circling overhead. Lifting his sweat filled eyes upward, Cooley yelled, "Come on, boys, here's some red meat for lunch!"

Sheriff Matt Blake watched, together with six Yaquis, as the platoon made its way back to the spring.

As Sergeant Cooley dismounted, Blake extended his right hand. "Name's Matt Blake. I'm sheriff over at Tucson."

"Jed Cooley," answered the sergeant, managing a smile, "out of Fort Simms."

"Aren't you boys a little way out of your territory?" queried Blake.

"Yeah, a little," answered Cooley with pain, "but we had to catch that bloodthirsty renegade."

"We'd better get you attended to," Blake said, looking hard at the bloodstained shirt.

While Corporal Todd and Private Palmer assisted the big

sergeant up the mount and disappeared behind the rocks, the remainder of the platoon began to walk amongst the Apache corpses scattered on the desert floor.

The blazing sun was sending down its rays in bolts of invisible fire, as it slowly lifted in the morning sky.

Numberless flies, seemingly coming from out of nowhere, were buzzing from corpse to corpse.

Matt Blake called to one of the soldiers who was examining a dead Apache nearby. "Have you men got a shovel with you?"

"We're not burying these savages!" the men retorted. "Let the buzzards have 'em!"

Blake lifted his eyes upward. The buzzards had finished circling. Narrowing his eyes against the sun's rays, he ran his gaze along the horizon. He looked in the direction where the sergeant had left Samanti. There they were, screeching, hopping, feasting.

"Don't want it for the Apaches," Blake answered, "need it to bury a friend!"

The soldier approached Blake. "We'll help you bury your friend, Sheriff," he said.

"Won't be necessary," replied Blake. "I would rather do it myself. Personal matter."

The soldier nodded, walked to a horse, and pulled a short-handled, sharp-pointed shovel from the pack. "Much obliged," said the sheriff. Carrying the shovel to a spot at the base of the tall slender rock, the tall man began digging.

As the soldiers moved among the corpses of men and horses, a wounded Apache buck, lying next to a dead pinto, regained consciousness. He could hear the soldiers talking to one another. Cautiously, he opened his eyes.

Ever so slowly, he turned his head, lifting it slightly. The voices were coming closer. His left shoulder was bleeding from a bullet sunk deep in the flesh. With his right hand, he slipped the knife from his side.

One of the men, a short, stocky private, was walking straight toward him. Holding his knife close to his body, he dropped his head and closed his eyes. While he held his breath, he could feel the white man's eyes on the back of his head. The soldier muttered something to himself and moved on. The Apache sprang to his feet. With one lunge, he sank the knife into the soldier's back, all the way to the hilt.

Four rifles barked almost in unison. The Indian was dead before he hit the ground. The knife had gone through the soldier's heart from the back side. He died in less than a minute.

"Take their knives and jam 'em through every one of 'em's neck!" one of the soldiers shouted. "Make sure every one of 'em is dead!"

Corporal Todd appeared at the top of the mount. "What happened?" he called.

"One of these skunks was still alive, Corporal. He knifed Sweeney! Killed him!"

Todd's head dropped. Lifting it again, he shouted, "Bring him up this way. We'll bury him!"

While Matt Blake took a break to down some water, he glanced at his prisoner. Duke McClain was still sitting where the sheriff had thrown him before the shooting started. All the starch had gone out of him. He sat there quietly, seemingly oblivious to the burning sun or what was going on around him.

Stepping back into the hole, now about a foot deep, he began to pitch dirt. Two of Cooley's men approached Blake, carrying Sweeney's body. "Wouldn't mind if we dug one next to you, would you, Sheriff?" one of them asked.

Without pausing, he answered in a kind but firm tone, "My friend was a Yaqui soldier. I doubt if your pardner would have wanted to be buried next to a red man." Pausing, he pointed the shovel handle to a clear spot about twenty yards away. "Why don't you bury him over by that clump of mesquite?"

"Sure, Sheriff," answered the soldier. "Probably be a little softer diggin' over there anyhow."

Matt Blake had a special reason for wanting only Gray Wolf at the base of the rock.

As he continued to dig, the three men emerged from the spring enclosure. Sergeant Cooley was wrapped in gauze around the middle. His shirt was open, hanging loose on his shoulders. He walked with a slight stoop, but was manipulating on his own power.

Blake glanced again at Duke. He was sitting in the same spot. A cigarette was dangling from the corner of his mouth as he continually poked his right index finger through the hole the sheriff had shot in his hat.

Cooley approached Blake, who continued tossing dirt on the ever-growing mound beside the grave. "This grave for the Yaqui by the pool, Sheriff?"

"Yep."

"Somethin' special to you?" he asked with a tender tone.

"Yep. Saved my life. Took two bullets Samanti meant for me."

"Some of 'em are really white men at heart," said Cooley.

Matt Blake frowned. Jamming the shovel into the hard earth so it would stand alone, he took off his hat and mopped his face and neck with a bandanna. "Fella could take that two ways, Sergeant."

Placing the Stetson back on his head, he continued, "I wonder who was really a white man at heart…Gray Wolf or Samanti."

As the big sergeant mopped his own face, Blake went on, "Gray Wolf called me his blood brother. I gave water and aid to him and his braves. They would have died otherwise. When he saw that all white eyes aren't greedy killers, he changed his mind. He was headed here to meet Samanti. They were going to plunder and murder white people together. Gray Wolf told me before he got here to the spring, he was calling it off with Samanti and going back home."

Blake pulled the shovel out of the sod. "The Indians have a legitimate reason to fight the whites, Sergeant. We invaded their land. By fighting us, they are merely doing what we would do if we were wearing their moccasins."

Cooley nodded his big red head in silent agreement.

"Trouble is," continued Blake, "some Indians become like white men. They get greedy and bloodthirsty. My job is necessary, Mr. Cooley, because white men are greedy and bloodthirsty. Samanti's defense of his land became twisted. He began to think like a white man. He and my prisoner over there," Blake nodded toward the little man with the finger through his hat, "are two of a kind. You had to rid this desert of Samanti. I have to rid the world of 'Mad-dog' McClain. He's going back to Tucson to stand trial and hang."

Jed Cooley tossed a glance toward McClain.

"So you see, sergeant," the sheriff concluded, "I would rather have it the way Gray Wolf saw it. As his adopted blood brother, he saw me a red man at heart."

"Must have been some man," Cooley said.

Matt Blake chuckled. "Sort of ironic, Mr. Cooley."

"Whaddya mean?"

"Just before Gray Wolf took my bullets, Samanti said that Gray Wolf was no longer an Indian. In my book, Samanti is the one that ceased to be the Indian."

Corporal Alex Todd approached the sergeant. "Smith says there's forty-three dead Apaches laying out there, Sarge. Plus six horses. Lucky we had 'em bottled up like that. Otherwise more of 'em would have got away."

"Yeah," replied Cooley. "With Samanti, that makes forty-four. How many you reckon got away?"

"Don't rightly know. I'd say at least a dozen. Maybe more. They didn't bother to gather up the stray horses. I saw a bunch of the pintos gathering together toward that bunch of red rocks," Todd said, pointing northwest.

"They probably won't go far," interjected Matt Blake. "They no doubt smelled the spring. They'll be wanting water."

"One thing fer sure, them Apaches won't try coming back

while we're here," said Cooley, "not without ammunition."

"How do you know they're out of ammunition?" asked Blake. He checked on McClain out of the corner of his eye.

"They shot it all up when we fought 'em a couple days ago," replied Cooley.

Matt Blake stopped digging, took off his hat, shaking his head back and forth. "That scoundrel!" he said, almost smiling.

"Samanti?" asked Todd, readjusting the sling on his arm.

"Yeah! He was bluffing us!" Blake mopped sweat. "You've got to say one thing for him. He was one sharp hombre."

The tall sheriff took a long drink from his canteen, then poured a generous portion over his head. Capping the canteen, he replaced his hat and returned to the task.

Sergeant Jed Cooley spoke to his corporal. "Alex, better have the men cut some meat off those dead horses. It'll be spoiled by tomorrow in this heat. We'll get one good meal off of them anyway."

"You might have your men dress out that antelope over there, Sergeant," Blake chimed in. "The Yaquis were just getting started when the trouble began."

Sergeant Cooley had not noticed the antelope. "Great!" he exclaimed. "Hey, Todd!"

The corporal had walked a good distance away. "Yeah, Sarge?" he shouted back.

"Sheriff, here, says there's an antelope needs dressing out," he shouted, pointing toward the dead animal.

The six Yaquis were behind the rocks at the spring. They were having their own private funeral service for Gray Wolf.

Their mournful chant lifted from the rocks to the ears of the white men.

While Matt Blake continued digging, he noticed that a cloud suddenly covered the sun. A breeze came. The sudden change made goose pimples rise all over his body. The respite from the sun's rays was a welcome relief. Looking into the sky, he saw more clouds forming from the west. They were dark.

"Rain sure would feel good," he said to himself.

By noon the sky was completely gray. As Matt climbed out of the finished grave, a strong wind was blowing. Duke McClain was on his feet, watching the soldiers cut the antelope meat into steaks. The sheriff remembered that he had not completed tying the outlaw's hands. Glancing about, he noticed that all the horses had been unsaddled, even his own and McClain's. Feeling certain that McClain would not try to bolt for freedom on bareback, he decided not to tie his hands till they were ready to leave.

The mournful chant was still echoing from the spring. Blake wondered how long the primitive ceremony would continue.

A voice spoke from behind him. "What are your plans, Sheriff?" It was big Jed Cooley.

"You mean about moving on?"

"Yeah."

"Figure to pull out as soon as I bury Gray Wolf. We can still make Tapanic Tank by sundown tomorrow, if we get going. You?"

"We'll camp here tonight. Pull out early in the morning. All that flesh will start stinking when the sun hits tomorrow.

It's gonna smell pretty bad."

Matt Blake had not noticed that the chanting had stopped, until Quiet Bear stood beside him.

"We are ready if you are," the Yaqui said in a somber tone.

"Yes," answered Blake. "Excuse me, Sergeant," he said, turning away.

Cooley nodded and gave a weak smile.

The wind whipped around the base of Indian Head rock, scattering sand against the blanketed body of Gray Wolf. The glowering sky grew darker as the six Yaquis tenderly lowered the body into the yawning hole.

Matt Blake stood at the head of the grave as the Yaquis lined its length, three on a side. They turned their stolid eyes toward the tall man. Except for the tears in his eyes, Quiet Bear thought that Blake's face resembled carved stone.

A gust of wind pelted sand against the wall of the tall rock towering overhead. The sheriff spoke above the howl of the wind. "If it were not for the courage of Gray Wolf and his devotion to me as his adopted blood brother, it would be my body placed beneath the sod instead of his."

Lifting his eyes upward to the wind-chiseled Indian head, he continued, "In His wisdom, the Great Spirit knew that one day this brave man would die here and be lowered into the earth which he and all Indians hold so sacred. By predetermined earthquakes, wind, and rain the Great Spirit formed this giant Indian Head rock as a monument to Gray Wolf. May his memory be fixed in our hearts as his monument is in this land."

All was quiet for a short moment. Suddenly, above the howling wind, the voice of Sergeant Jed Cooley barked a quick command. Matt Blake raised his line of sight in time to see seven soldiers lift their rifles, point them toward the heavy sky, and respond to three commands of "Fire!" in succession.

Blake's eyes met those of Quiet Bear. The sheriff smiled thinly. Quiet Bear's lips remained the same, but Blake detected a smile in his eyes. The other Yaquis looked at the sheriff. Blake knew the old traditional line that Indians do not cry. When the sound of the bugle playing taps filtered through the wind, through his own tears the tall lawman saw the colorless streams on six red faces.

Little drops of rain began to speckle the dusty ground. Jed Cooley dispatched two men to saddle Blake's and McClain's horses. The gray was once again burdened with water, grain, and supplies.

After the sheriff had tied the sullen outlaw's hands, he said his goodbyes. As he shook hands with Sergeant Cooley, he said, "Thanks Cooley…for the military honors you bestowed on my friend."

The big sergeant smiled without showing his teeth and nodded his head.

"We go home, now," Quiet Bear said.

"That's good," replied Blake, as they shook hands Indian style.

Little drops of rain washed Quiet Bear's face as he said his last words to the sheriff. "You…Yaqui blood brother."

CHAPTER EIGHT

It was raining hard as Matt Blake and Duke McClain rode out of Indian Head Spring. Just before they passed over a sharp bluff about two miles out, the sheriff reined his horse and looked back. There stood Gray Wolf's monument, tall and erect. Blake swallowed a hot lump and clucked to the dun.

Both men were soaked to the skin, but it felt so good compared to the usual unbearable heat, neither complained.

Matt Blake thought of the remaining dozen or so Apaches. One of the soldiers had remarked that Hondo escaped alive. The small band would now look to him as their leader. Would they return to their villages? Or would they carry out Samanti's nefarious plan? The nearest water was at Yuma. Certainly they would not chance appearing there. The next nearest water would be Tapanic Tank. The Apaches had no ammunition, but still they were dangerous. He thought of the two wagons ahead of him on the trail.

Hondo and his men would be on the warpath after the slaughter at Indian Head Spring. He hoped that whoever was traveling in the wagons was well armed. The Apaches would probably evade traveling the established trail between Indian

Head Spring and Tapanic Tank. He hoped that the Indians would somehow miss seeing the wagons.

The rain was coming down hard. Any signs left on the trail would vanish under the heavy torrent.

Duke McClain rode in absolute silence. He knew that with every step his horse took, his chances of escape grew slimmer. He relived the nightmare. He thought of the crude gallows, the beckoning fingers, the mocking laughter. He thought of the eyes, those hollow white pools. A shudder went over him. He shook his head, trying to cast off this train of thought.

Almost without thinking, the outlaw reached in his shirt pocket for his tobacco. He cursed when it lay in his hand, soaking wet.

Matt Blake heard the words, but did not distinguish them. "What say?" he shouted over the rain.

"Nuthin!" muttered McClain, his head hung low.

The hours passed in soaking monotony. By late afternoon the rain eased off. The wind died down. About an hour before dark, the rain stopped and the clouds overhead began to dissipate.

Matt Blake began to scan the moistened desert for a camp spot. About a mile ahead, he saw a cluster of boulders. "We'll stop up there," he said, pointing.

McClain grunted an acknowledgement with a noticeable lack of enthusiasm.

Approaching the desired spot, the tall sheriff dismounted a few yards out. Slipping the Winchester from its boot, he told McClain to dismount and follow him.

"I ain't goin' in there until you make sure it's safe," the outlaw argued.

"I'm not leaving you here to run off with the horses," Blake retorted.

"I said I ain't goin' in there."

"You've got a choice," said Blake. "You can lay here in the mud with a pistol welt on your head…or you can walk in those rocks with me."

"All right. All right. Let's get it over with," McClain said.

A thorough search revealed an unoccupied site inside the rock circle about fifteen yards square. There was a slight hint of red on the western horizon as Matt Blake set up camp. After tending to the three animals, he looked among the mesquite for dry wood.

He opened a can of beans, unwrapped some jerky, and poured some water from one of the canteens. "No fire tonight, Duke," he said to the outlaw who was perched on a wet rock, "everything is soaked."

Night fell over the desert like a thick blanket. After tying the outlaw with the waist-band rope, Matt Blake stretched out on the damp sand. McClain was asleep almost immediately.

The lawman looked up at the star-studded sky. He thought of Gray Wolf. A queasy feeling swept over him. Death had brushed close to him, only to sink its fangs into his newfound Indian friend. It seemed that he had known Gray Wolf all his life, yet it had been only two days.

Biting down hard, he relived the bloody battle of that morning. Again and again, he saw Gray Wolf leap in front of the rifle. He thought he could smell the dust, the gunsmoke, the blood. Coming back to the present, he was aware of the sweet, clean smell of the desert. The rain had washed everything clean.

Listening to the steady breathing of the outlaw, he thought of Tucson. The trial would not take long. Duke would be convicted by the testimony of the eye-witnesses who saw him gun down Margie Kendall in cold blood. Judge Peterson would probably give him a few days to sweat it out before the hanging.

He thought of getting back to his office, back to some semblance of a routine. Back to—Wiley Chance! Hal Stedman! It shocked him that thoughts of his two faithful deputies had not crossed his mind since he left Yuma. He hoped things were quiet in Tucson. Not that those two could not handle whatever came along. Wiley—bless his ole heart. He could almost outdraw his boss. Hal wasn't far behind. Good men.

Morning came, so clear that the distant mountains far to the northwest seemed close and sharply etched against the horizon. By the time the tall sheriff had fed his prisoner a cold breakfast and prepared to leave, he could already feel the promise of heat.

Swinging his legs over the saddle, Blake looked soberly at McClain astride the bay. Aiming the dun's nose toward the opening of the rock enclosure, he said, "Let's go."

"You ain't goin' nowhere, Sheriff!"

The husky voice came from atop one of the boulders. It was Rob Chamberlain.

"Reach!" barked another voice, from the opposite side. Will Nichols' face was twisted with a wry smile.

Duke McClain's countenance lifted. He let out a high-pitched squeal, which evolved into a shout.

Matt Blake spun his head back and forth, eyeing the two rifle muzzles that were trained on him.

"I said reach, lawman!" Nichols shouted.

Slowly the tall man's hands climbed skyward.

Duke McClain leaped from his horse. Laughing with ecstatic glee, he lifted Blake's .45 from its holster. By the time he had yanked the sheriff's rifle from its scabbard, Rob Chamberlain was standing on the ground beside McClain. "Git this rope off me," McClain said to Chamberlain, extending his wrists. In a moment, the rope dropped to the ground.

"Come on down," Chamberlain shouted to Nichols, who was already scrambling from the rock.

McClain jammed the sheriff's revolver under his belt, handed the rifle to Chamberlain, and tore into the saddlebag containing his revolver. Breaking it open, he hissed at Blake, "When it's emptied this time, it'll be into your gut!"

After loading the revolver, McClain spun it on his finger, slipping it into his holster. Turning to his friends, he said, "Soon as I kill this jackal on the dun, you boys are gonna tell me all about how you found us!"

Matt Blake's mouth went dry. He had been in tight spots before, but it would take a miracle to get him out of this one.

"Shoot 'im and get it over with, Duke," Nichols retorted. "We can talk later. Let's get outta here!"

"Get off the horse," McClain commanded Blake.

The tall man swung his right leg over the pommel and slid to the earth, never taking his eyes from McClain.

Duke snarled. "We ain't in that big of a hurry, boys. I owe the lawman. I aim to pay." Pulling Blake's revolver from his belt, he said, "You boys cover him while I have some fun. If you have to shoot him, just wing him. Ain't nobody gonna kill him but me."

It was plain to Matt Blake that Chamberlain and Nichols were anxious to hit the trail. Reluctantly, they leveled their rifles at the sheriff.

"Git it over with," Chamberlain said.

Matt Blake wondered which one would win an ugly contest, Chamberlain or McClain. Each was hideous in his own way. It actually was a standoff in contrast. Where McClain's eyes were narrow-set and beady, the other man's eyes were set wide apart and large…almost perfectly round. McClain's sharp nose was hooked like an eagle's beak. Chamberlain's nose was broad and flat. Blake thought that he resembled a bulldog he had seen once.

Suddenly, McClain's arm swung upward in an arc. He brought the revolver down hard on Blake's left temple. The tall man staggered, trying to keep his feet. The outlaw hit him again in the same place.

Matt Blake felt his legs weaken. They refused to support him any longer. The ground seemed to fly up and hit him. He felt a boot, swung hard, hit his left jawbone. Now his ribs were caving in. He sucked hard to get his breath. Blood was flowing into his left eye. As he blinked against the blood, his right eye saw the gun barrel flash in the sun. He felt it crush against his skull. It felt like a deep, dark whirlpool was pulling him down into a black pit.

All sense of time had left him when Matt Blake felt the hot sun on his back. Voices kept fading in and out. Sharp barbs of pain began to announce their presence. The idea of moving anything seemed beyond possibility.

The voices were beginning to articulate into words. Suddenly he knew where he was. It all came back in a flash. Without opening his eyes or moving a muscle, Blake strained his ears.

The husky voice of Rob Chamberlain was saying, "So we watched the whole thing from some rocks about half a mile away. Those Apaches were dropping like flies."

"You should've seen what that big sergeant did to one of them Indians," interjected Nichols. "Busted him up somethin' terrible, then heaved him on a cactus patch. Whew! We weren't a hunnerd feet away. It was so bad, even some of them soldiers got sick."

"So we decided to lay back till you were a long ways from the spring before we rescued you," Chamberlain added.

No one spoke for several moments. Matt Blake felt as if his back was on fire. The sun was merciless. Then the silence was broken.

"Why don't you just shoot 'im now and get it over with?" asked Will Nichols.

"'Cause I want him to see it comin'!" McClain barked.

Matt wanted to shake his head. The cobwebs were heavy. He knew if he did, they would know he was awake. He needed time to think. Think! With flames dancing on his back and a thousand red-hot irons jabbed into his body?

The voices. Something was different about their speech. He listened hard. Chamberlain was talking now. "There's a couple of wagons travelin' a day or so ahead of us. We can probably replenish our food supply. Take anything else we want, too."

"Maybe get some more likker!" said McClain.

Liquor! That's it. There was a slight slur to their speech. The two outlaws had whiskey with them. They probably started drinking when the whirlpool sucked him into that pit. McClain sounded as if he had taken in the most.

"Time he was wakin' up," said Nichols. A heavy boot rolled Blake's face up. The pain stabbed through his body. An unsolicited cry escaped his lips.

"Hey, fellas! He's awake!" cried Nichols.

Blake felt rough hands under his armpits. He tried to open his eyes. The left one refused. Dried blood had sealed it shut. As the right one revealed a flash of sunlight, he felt a wave of nausea sweep over him.

Duke slapped Blake's face. The sting seemed to clear away some of the cobwebs that hung from wall to wall in his brain.

Blake opened his right eye. He was suddenly aware that his head was hanging back. He was looking at a clear, unclouded sky. His head was jerked violently downward. Blinking the eye, he saw the sweaty, ugly face of Duke McClain. The outlaw was holding Blake's jaws between the thumb and fingers of his hand.

Shaking the bloody face, he spoke with authority. "Yer gonna walk a ways. Now, Sheriff."

"Whassya talkin' about?" Chamberlain asked, a note of disgust in his tone.

"Don't want to kill him here," McClain retorted. "Some travelers might camp here, like we did, and find his body. They'd bury it. I want the buzzards to eat him."

Almost without realizing it, Sheriff Matt Blake was walking on the level desert floor. His feet felt like lead. The sun was vicious.

The three outlaws were riding behind him. His head was spinning. Nausea came and went in waves. Suddenly the ground flew up and hit him again.

"Just a little further, lawman," said McClain, lifting Blake to his feet.

Soon the sheriff found himself standing on the edge of a draw. Sharply sloped, it was about twenty feet deep. A strong hand spun him around, putting the draw at his heels.

The ground all about this area was covered with small chunks of black lava, long cooled since the days of live volcanoes.

The whiskey had taken effect on Duke McClain. His eyes were red and glassy. Looking to the bottom of the draw, he said with a slur, "Nobody will find him down there. The buzzards can pick his bones clean."

McClain laughed as he turned his back and walked a wobbly ten paces, counting them off audibly. Chamberlain and Nichols sat on their horses and watched with a cold devil-may-care attitude. The yellow-haired outlaw turned around. "You fellas think I can blow his head off at ten paces? Huh? Do ya?"

"Sure, Duke," replied Chamberlain. "Will you just git it done? We gotta ketch them there wagons."

Matt Blake stood wavering, the draw to his back. There was nothing he could do. He was at the outlaw's mercy.

"I need a little water," McClain said. He walked a crooked line to Blake's dun, lifted the canteen from the saddle, and began to drink. Water was running down his chin, spotting his shirt and vest.

The sheriff ran his dry tongue over his parched lips.

"Want some water, Mr. Tall Man?" McClain asked, slurring his words.

Blake's head wound was bleeding again. Sweat and blood ran freely down the left side of his face. His knees were getting weaker. He would soon fall to the earth again.

"Here, Mr. Tall Man," McClain said, tossing the canteen within ten feet of the sheriff. Matt Blake took a step forward, reaching downward. The canteen had fallen against a small cluster of lava, leaving it on a tilt. As the sheriff reached for the canteen, McClain's .44 roared. The canteen bucked as the bullet ripped through it, exposing a jagged hole. The water spurted, then began to bubble into the ground.

Blake licked his dry lips again. All the moisture seemed drained from his body.

"Get back where you were!" McClain shouted. The gun roared again. Lava rocks and dirt spewed at Blake's feet. The sheriff made his way back to the edge of the draw. His knees almost gave way as he turned to face "Mad-dog."

Noticing the sheriff's knees buckle, McClain laughed heartily.

"Whatsa matter, Blake? Scared to die?"

Blake did not answer.

"If you know any prayers, lawman, better git to sayin' 'em. I'll give you two minutes!"

Blake remained silent.

"Ain't gonna pray, eh?"

"If you're going to kill me, Duke, get it done. I'm not going to grovel for you." Blake's one open eye was steel blue. It showed no fear.

"Tell you what I'm gonna do, Sheriff," McClain said with a heavy tongue. "I'm gonna will my noose to you! You do remember that noose you promised me, don't you?

Blake's head was getting clearer now. The complete vision had returned to the right eye. The left one was still matted shut with caked blood.

"Remember when I thought you might shoot me out of the saddle the other day, Blake? Remember? Remember I said if you shoot me, I wouldn't wear that noose? Remember?"

Matt Blake remembered. He said nothing.

"Remember I said they don't hang dead men? Remember I asked you what good is a dead man's noose? Well, Mr. Lawman, I'm willin' that dead man's noose to you—'cause you're a dead man!"

The .44 roared. Matt Blake's head snapped back. His body rolled down the steep embankment of volcanic rock fragments.

Duke McClain ran in a crooked line to the edge of the draw. The sheriff lay face up, eyes closed. The outlaw stood staring through whiskey-sodden eyes at the round black hole on the left corner of Blake's forehead. Blood trickled from it.

"Come on, Duke, let's git goin!" Rob Chamberlain said.

Duke McClain laughed as he mounted the big dun. Not only had he taken Matt Blake's life, but he now had his horse and his guns.

"Let's go, boys!" he shouted.

Leading his own bay and the gray bearing water and supplies, McClain urged the dun in the direction of Tapanic Tank. It was nearly noon. McClain recalled the sheriff saying that the tank was a good day's ride from where they had camped.

As the sun bore down on the three outlaws, the dust began to rise. The day wore on. No one had spoken a word for over an hour, when suddenly Will Nichols lifted his hand and pointed to a shallow arroyo just ahead.

"Them two wagons camped right up here last night," he said.

The trio dismounted and examined the campsite.

"Can't tell how many people travelin', but there's both male and female," mused Duke McClain. "Adults. No kids. One person is riding horseback."

"We'll catch 'em before they get to the tank, if we ride till midnight, then get an early start in the mornin'," said Nichols. A brief discussion led to an agreement on Nichols' suggestion. They mounted after watering the horses and continued eastward, the sun casting ebony shadows in their path. The western sky flamed from the lowering sun, then played with dusk.

The desert lay enveloped in a Stygian darkness for nearly

half an hour before the moon lifted a bright orange rim over the eastern horizon. By midnight, it hung in the sky like a giant silver disk.

The three outlaws slept, basking in the silver hue.

Matt Blake was not sure which came first. The mental knowledge that he was still in the world or the physical awareness of the stabbing pain in his forehead.

A large buzzard, after a cautious approach, took the motionless form for dead and began pecking at the black piece of lava rock which stuck to the blood on his forehead. It was a piece of rock which had deceived the bleary eyes of Duke McClain. It had appeared as a bullet hole from which blood was flowing.

The bullet had actually struck the left side of his forehead at a blunt angle and gouged a deep furrow across his scalp where the white skull bone showed clearly.

With the first two or three flicks of its beak, the buzzard dislodged the rock. The sharp pain of the beak on the open flesh and bone brought the sheriff's right eye open. The repulsive face of the buzzard suddenly came into focus. Blake's arms began to flail wildly. The frightened bird screeched and leaped backward, rustling his giant wings.

Matt Blake sat up quickly, still waving his arms and screaming at the ugly black buzzard. There was a savage, thunderous pounding inside his head. It felt like it was going to burst. The sun-bleached desert was whirling around him.

Carefully he lay his head back on the hot rocks. After a

few moments, he opened the one functioning eye again. The dizziness was subsiding. The pounding continued. Suddenly he was aware of a sliver of live fire that blazed along his throbbing head.

The buzzard had joined his cohorts in the brassy sky. The huge broad-winged carrion eaters were circling patiently overhead.

For several moments the tall man struggled to get on his feet. Standing erect, a wave of nausea claimed him. It soon passed. He rubbed at the blind left eye.

"Blood's dried over it," he said to himself.

Running his fingers back from his eye, he winced as they touched the open wound left by McClain's bullet.

McClain!

His head suddenly cleared. There was blood on the tips of his fingers. "I've got to go after that dirty killer!" The blood. "Got to stop that blood."

Slowly he pulled his shirttail from under his belt. "Mighty weak," he mumbled, as he labored to rip it in a long strip. Successful after several attempts, he wrapped it around his head and tied it.

Taking a few faltering steps, he looked out of the draw toward the rise where Duke had shot him. Squeezing his eyelids down to a slit, trying to minimize the sun's painful glare, he forced his legs to carry him up the steep slope.

Arriving at the top after a struggle, the open eye fell on his Stetson. Placing it on his head at an angle, he was thankful for the shade it afforded his throbbing head. The buzzards were screeching overhead. Looking skyward, he saw their heinous eyes watching him. Shaking his fist at them, he screamed, "I'll not die for you or buzzards like you!"

He lowered his face, blinking at slow intervals to relieve the temporary blindness imposed by the sun's harsh glare. His line of sight fell on the bullet-ridden canteen.

His mouth felt like a hot sand pit. The thought of the water once contained in that canteen intensified his thirst. He stared at it bitterly. He thought of Tapanic Tank, some thirty miles away. He could make it, he thought, if only he had water in that canteen. Otherwise…

He was reluctant to take his eye off the canteen. Something kept picking at his mind. A little cry escaped his lips as the realization came home. The canteen lay at an angle, propped upward on a small cluster of lava. The bullet hole that was visible was a good three inches from the bottom. The hole on the other side would be no lower.

He could hear the life-giving liquid slosh inside as he picked it up. He put the bullet hole to his lips, tilting his head. Matt Blake would not waste a drop of the precious water. It was hot and brackish, but it was wet. With five or six swallows, he could feel a new surge of strength.

Using just a little of the precious liquid, he daubed at his blood-caked left eye until it came open. Within a quarter of an hour, the tall man with the star still clinging to his dirty, tattered shirt was on his way toward Tapanic Tank. The bleeding wound underneath the cloth strip felt like a thousand little demons were raking it with coals of fire. Still he pushed on, taking brief respite now and then in the spotted shade of mesquite and other sparse desert shrubs.

Matt Blake slowly moved through a burning land of giant, grotesque saguaro cactus, green-trunked paloverde trees, mesquite, ocotillo, and little else. The stubborn sun bore down in fiery torrents. He allowed himself frequent small sips of water from the canteen. The strap was slung over his neck, but he was also careful to support it with one hand to keep any water from escaping through the bullet holes.

He thought of Hondo and his small band of renegades. If they found him out here, he would be tortured and finally put to death. Closing his red-rimmed eyes, he put Hondo from his thoughts.

Nothing stirred anywhere around him except eight or ten buzzards circling soundlessly in the brassy atmosphere overhead. "They'll have to eat something else," he said to himself with determination. "I'm going to make it back to Tucson somehow."

Matt Blake thought of Duke McClain. Where would he and his vile friends go? Utah? New Mexico? Colorado? Mexico? Oh, no! Not Mexico! His chances of ever bringing them to justice would grow mighty slim if they left the States or the Territories.

Right now, the nefarious trio was following the two wagons toward Tapanic Tank. He shuddered as he thought of what they would do to the travelers in the wagons.

Looking up at the wheeling buzzards, he thought of how their purpose and his were similar. Was he not a prowling scavenger, removing carrion such as "Mad-dog" McClain from the earth? It was his job, just as it was the task of the ugly birds, to rid the earth of rotting carcasses. He thought of their persistence. They would trail him, patiently, skillfully, until he fell. He realized he must be just as skillful, patient, and persistent in his task.

He was just about to stop and rest when he caught a distant movement in the corner of his eye. Indians! There were about a dozen riding eastward some two miles south. Peering through squinted eyes, he tried to focus clearly enough to tell if it was Hondo and his band. Too far. He could not tell. Soon they disappeared behind some bluffs. Taking the intended rest, he soon found himself on the move again.

The tracks of the three outlaws were following those of the wagons without wavering.

Matt Blake was suddenly aware that his shadow was stretching long before him. The treacherous sun would set soon. He wished for the strength to continue on after dark, but his wobbly legs telegraphed the message to his brain that it would not be. He must rest for the night.

Dusk came on swiftly. The sun cast purplish shadows behind the surrounding rocks. As it hung low over the rim of the earth, it flooded the sky with dazzling colors.

The weary lawman found a cluster of mesquite trees next to a large boulder. Sitting down with a sigh, he braced his back against the rock and rested his head on it. Closing his eyes, he felt the cool evening breeze on his blistered face. He had lain unconscious in the lava-strewn draw with his face upward. Even though he was deeply tanned, the concentrated rays of the sun had raised burning blisters. He was glad for one thing—the bleeding had stopped.

Soon darkness covered the desert. Rolling his head against

the rock, the sheriff opened his eyes. The moon was lifting its bright orange rim over the eastern horizon. Rising to his feet, Blake scanned the desert around him. The moon's soft light made the giant saguaros appear as menacing monsters, lurking in a strange and forbidding land.

The tall man sloshed the water in the canteen, taking a mental measurement of its dwindling supply. He estimated that he had covered about ten miles since he had started walking.

"Twenty more miles," he said. He balanced the canteen in his hand. "Don't know, I think I better get up early and make tracks while it's still cool." His throat felt dry. He would allow himself just one small swallow before going to sleep. As the blessed moisture from the bullet hole met his lips, he fought back the desire to gulp down the rest of it. Lowering the canteen, he rolled the water in his mouth for a long moment, then slowly swallowed…

Matt Blake awakened long before dawn. The moon was low in the western sky, casting its silver rays on a few long-fingered clouds. He lifted his stiff body upward. The first few steps were a bit painful, but the pain soon subsided with movement.

His stomach reminded him that it had been sorely neglected. He thought of his usual breakfast every morning at Maude's Café in Tucson. Blistering hot black coffee, eggs, steak, potatoes, buckwheat cakes, maple syrup. "Got to think of something else," he told himself.

The rest had helped. Even with the lack of food his legs felt stronger. He would make it to Tapanic Tank today. He had made no plans as to how he would make it on to Tucson. All concentration now was on getting to the big pool of water.

The sun peeked over the horizon at the tall man. He adjusted the canteen strap on his shoulder. He knew the desert must be met at its own tempo if he was to survive, so he moved with a steady, easy stride.

As he approached a shallow arroyo, he came to an abrupt halt. Kneeling down, he studied the marks on the ground. The two wagons had camped here. Moving away from the spot where McClain and his henchmen had stopped to study the campsite, he calculated that there were at least two women and one man. No children. One woman was heavier than the other woman. Although their footprints were the same size, one set imprinted the dust deeper than the other. Matt Blake did not know it, but Duke McClain's overlooking the depth of the feminine footprints would save his life and that of the smaller woman.

The sun grew hotter as it lifted higher. Soon the heat was like a blanket. He swallowed some more of the brackish water and trudged on, a pitiful moving speck in an infinity of blazing desert.

The buzzards returned. His continuous movement had not discouraged them in the least. He thought of the horror of awakening in the blistering draw and looking into the face of the hideous buzzard. He doubted that the awful picture would ever fade from his memory.

By midday, his strength was quickly dissipating. His legs were getting weak. Dropping to his knees beside a mesquite tree, he rolled into its shade. After several minutes, he tilted the canteen, putting his lips to the bullet hole. Nothing! It was empty. A wave of panic swept over him.

"No. No. Must not lose control," he told himself. "Got to make it."

He crawled out from under the tree. Standing to his feet, he glanced at the west. Swinging his gaze eastward, he mumbled to himself, "About twelve miles to go." The tall sheriff forced himself forward. From time to time, his eyes fell on the tracks beneath his feet. He came upon the spot where the three outlaws had slept. They had not built a fire. They probably were taking no chances on alerting the people in the wagons of their presence.

Bolts of invisible fire were shooting through him. The sun showed no mercy. The scattered heat-blasted cacti, starving mesquite, and brittle creosote bushes seemed to join in chorus to warn the weakening man of his impending fate in this infinity of blistering sand.

Matt Blake sleeved away the sweat from his brow, knocking his hat loose. It fell to the ground. As he bent over to pick it up, dizziness swept over him. He straightened up, dropped the hat, and fell stiff-legged, head first.

When consciousness alerted his senses, he opened his eyes. The glare bit into his head. He blinked several times, adjusting his eyes to the brightness around him. From the position of the sun, he guessed he had been out for over an hour.

He clawed at his throat. It was on fire. Water! He must have water. How far to the tank? His head was spinning. "Can't stop. Got to make it."

Red liquid was flowing into his left eye. The wound had opened again when he fell. Calling on every reserve in his system, he pressed on.

Looking up ahead, the determined lawman saw the land lifting upward to a crest. The tracks were still beneath his feet. The crest was topped with giant white boulders. As he slowly came abreast of the crest, he staggered to one of the boulders, leaning against it.

Looking down the slope ahead of him, he saw more giant boulders nestled in a virtual forest of paloverde trees. Something among the trees caught his attention. He squinted. There seemed to be a gray film over his eyes.

His feet were taking him down the slope. "Is that…is that…a wagon?"

The world was fading away. Everything was losing its color. The earth jerked itself from beneath him. An inklike darkness enfolded him.

CHAPTER NINE

The happy birds in the paloverde trees were singing their desert ballads when sound invaded Matt Blake's pit of darkness.

As his eyes opened, he saw a shadow silhouetted against the sky. He remembered the ghastly buzzard which had stood over him before. He closed and opened his eyes several times, trying to clear his vision.

Suddenly a face came into focus. He blinked again. The morning sunlight seemed to dance on her golden hair. He looked into her eyes. They were smiling, along with her ruby-red lips. Not painted, he noted. Just a natural ruby-red. He had never seen such green eyes; two shining pools of emerald green, so full, so soft and tender. He knew that somewhere he had seen lips like hers before. Oh yes. In a painting on some-one's parlor wall.

Her nose was thin and stately, perfectly proportioned for the graceful lines of her face. The hair that outlined her face had the appearance of spun gold, like the sun when it slipped up on the eastern horizon, shattering the shades of night.

Her lips slowly parted. "Good morning."

My voice. Where's my voice? Matt Blake struggled to

force air past his vocal chords. "G-good morning."

"I think you're going to make it," she said, smiling.

His hand went to his wounded head. It was wrapped tightly. The aroma of hot coffee drifted past his nose. Turning his head, he saw the coffee pot through the spokes of a wagon wheel. Then it all came back. He remembered seeing the wagon among the trees in the early afternoon sun.

Wait a minute. Did she say morning? Lifting his eyes skyward, he could see the morning sun through the trees.

Recognizing his confusion, she said, "I found you yesterday afternoon. Do you think you can sit up?"

With tender but firm hands, she helped him into a sitting position, placing his back to the wagon wheel. "Bet you're hungry, Sheriff."

A startled look crossed his face. "Oh, you saw my badge."

"Didn't need it," she said. "I recognized you the moment I saw you."

"Do we know each other?"

"Not exactly," she said, shifting her eyes downward.

"Are you from Tucson?"

"No. Temple Flats."

"Oh, yeah. Little town about forty miles south."

"Uh-huh." Jumping to her feet, she said, "I'll fix you some breakfast."

Matt Blake scanned the area. There were two wagons, two teams, and a riding horse. The horses were tethered about thirty yards from the wagons. He looked about for the other people. Her back was toward him as she bent over the fire.

"Where's everybody else?" he asked.

Her shoulders slumped. She stopped what she was doing. Sensing that something was wrong, he gripped the wagon wheel and pulled himself to his feet. His legs felt like boiled mush. Staggering to her, he placed a hand on her shoulder. She tilted her face upward, looking into his eyes. Tears were starting down her cheeks. She stood up, steadying the tall man.

"They're dead," she said through thin, drawn lips.

"What happened?"

"Three men…" She swallowed hard. "Three men jumped us just about this time yesterday morning."

Blake bit his lip. He did not have to ask for their description.

"They killed Ma and Pa Lind…and Uncle Jake." She was fighting to retain her composure. "I've been working on their graves," she said, pointing to an open area some twenty yards away.

The sheriff followed her finger. There were three shapeless forms lying on the ground, covered with blankets. One grave was dug. Another one started.

Matt Blake looked down at her as she brushed the tears from her cheeks. He had noticed that she was a small woman, but at this moment, she seemed even smaller. He wondered if they had harmed her, why she was spared and the others murdered.

"Did they harm you, ma'am?" he asked.

"No," she said, taking a deep breath. "They didn't see me." Turning toward the fire, she said, "Let's get some food into you and I'll tell you about it."

While he wolfed down his breakfast of flapjacks, hardtack, beef jerky, and several cups of coffee, the golden-haired lady told the story.

The three outlaws had apparently come upon the wagons quite suddenly. Matt Blake could understand this, having topped the ridge and spotted the wagon almost instantly the day before. They had not lain back and observed the campers. If they had, they would have known there were two women.

The younger woman, now telling Matt Blake the story, had taken a bucket of water and walked a good distance into the trees. Finding a spot behind a large boulder, she had disrobed and bathed. She was just finishing buttoning her dress when she heard loud voices coming from the campsite.

Peering over the boulder through the trees, she saw the three outlaws holding the two elderly men and the old woman at gunpoint. The two larger men ransacked the wagons, taking food and guns, while the little slender one with the beak nose and jagged Adam's apple shouted threats at the old folks.

Having loaded down their pack horse, the three men mounted up. While laughing gleefully, the smaller man emptied his revolver into the elderly travelers. The outlaws rode away in a cloud of dust.

All three victims were dead when she got to them.

Matt Blake pointed out how fortunate she had been, first in the timing of her bath and second, that the outlaws had come over the ridge and apparently had been spotted by someone in the camp, leaving no time for hidden observation.

Recalling the wagons' previous campsite, the sheriff queried as to why they stopped so early the previous afternoon before the killings. Certainly they could have made it to Tapanic Tank before dark. She explained that Uncle Jake was not feeling well, so they had stopped for his sake. Knowing the Tank was less than ten miles away and planning to spend the night there, they were in no hurry to pull out on the fateful morning.

A new surge of burning hatred for Duke McClain shot like thunderbolts through Sheriff Matt Blake.

"It was late afternoon when I ran out of strength, left off my grave digging, and returned to the wagons," the golden-haired lady was saying. "I saw several buzzards hovering and when one of them swooped low, I saw you lying there."

"I sure am grateful, ma'am," he said. "I probably would have died right there."

It occurred to Matt Blake that he did not even know the lady's name. "Pardon me, ma'am, but I haven't even asked you your name."

She had been looking into his eyes. Suddenly she was looking at the ground. Nervously, she met his gaze again. "Holly Lind."

Holly Lind. Lind…Lind. A little bell was making an uncertain sound somewhere in Matt Blake's belfry. He studied her face. She would be in her early thirties…

Hank Lind!

Holly saw the recognition come over the sheriff's countenance.

"Hank Lind was my husband, Sheriff Blake."

His mind flashed back. Five-six years ago. He had arrested four bank robbers. Several people had been killed in a shoot-out in a Tucson bank. The four men were brought to trial. Hank Lind had participated in the holdup, but witnesses testified that he had done none of the killing.

The other three robbers were hung. Lind was sentenced to life in Yuma Territorial Prison for having a part in a robbery in which people were killed.

"I remember that Lind's wife was at the trial," Blake said, "but I don't remember seeing her."

"I was just a face in the crowd, Mr. Blake."

The tall man was noticeably uncomfortable. He was now having trouble meeting her gaze. "You said that Hank Lind was your husband?"

"Yes. He died two weeks ago. Scurvy. Prison food isn't much," she said.

"I'm terribly sorry, ma'am," Blake said.

"Thank you, Sheriff," she answered, "but it's not what it might appear at first. Hank destroyed everything that was between us when he turned bad."

Holly's pretty face was grim as she told Matt Blake the story. George Lind, whose body now lay beneath a blanket under the nearby trees, was proprietor of the general store in Temple Flats, a small mining town north of Tucson. Holly's father, a miner, had moved his family to Temple Flats when she was eighteen. Hank worked for his father in the store.

After Hank and Holly were married, he began to drink heavily. He would leave the saloon only when forced to at closing time. Many a morning she had found him passed out in one of the town's three streets. Things went from bad to worse. Hank began to ride off for days at a time with three strangers he had met one day at the saloon.

Reports were coming in from neighboring towns of four masked men holding up banks, stores, and stagecoaches. Hank seemed to have a lot of folding money. At Holly's inquiry, he passed it off as poker winnings.

One night when she was expecting their first child, he came home drunk. She tried to reason with him. He was breaking his parents' hearts. She did not want her child brought up in a drunkard's home. In a fit of anger, he knocked her down, kicking her savagely. She lost the child. The doctor told her she could never have any more.

The loss of the child seemed to have its effect on Hank. He stopped drinking. Forsaking the saloon, he began spending his evenings at home. It turned out to be only temporary. Within a month he was back on the bottle. He continued his mysterious, unexplained rides.

Holly's nerves were at the breaking point. Her love for Hank was dying. Their marriage was in a shambles. She decided to make one last desperate effort to hold it together. Returning from one of his escapades, he walked into the house with a sack full of money. She asked him to please sit down and discuss their faltering marriage.

"Marriage? What marriage? Ain't no marriage when a woman can't even give her husband a son!" he had shouted.

Holly felt the words form into a sword of ice that cut through her heart. When the coldness went away, the last embers of her love for Hank had died.

"He left with those words. The next time I heard of his whereabouts was when you jailed him in Tucson, over two years later."

Matt Blake noticed the sun climbing higher in the sky.

"I went to the trial for Ma and Pa Lind's sake," Holly continued. "When Hank received the life sentence, Pa sold the store. He and Ma would move to Yuma. They wanted to be near their son. My parents both died in the same year. The year after Hank ran away.

"I had no one. My sister, Lucy, had married and moved to Denver. I decided to go on to Yuma with Hank's parents. Pa's older brother, Jake, was a bachelor. He went along, too. Pa opened a store in Yuma. He and Ma were able to visit Hank twice a month, that is, except when he was in solitary."

Holly Lind lifted her shoulders and sighed, as if she had just unloaded a heavy burden.

"Then two weeks ago the superintendent of the prison walked into the store and told Pa that Hank was dead. And now, this," she said, looking toward the covered corpses. Again she wept.

Gaining control once again, she continued. "Ma and Pa decided to move back to Temple Flats. Pa sold the store last week and we packed up and headed east."

"What are you going to do now?" the sheriff asked.

"I haven't given it any thought, Mr. Blake."

"Tell you what. You can stay in Tucson till you make up your mind. I have a house. You can stay there as long as you want. I've got a bunk at the office."

"Oh, no. I couldn't put you out. I've got a little money, I

could…" Holly jumped to her feet and ran to the nearest wagon. Climbing into it, she threw open the lid of a small trunk. A shrill cry escaped her lips. "It's gone. Those dirty killers took my money!"

By this time, Matt Blake, who was feeling strength from his breakfast, was standing beside the wagon. He offered his arm. Slowly she stepped to the ground.

"I worked as a cook in the Sunset Café in Yuma," she said. "Saved up some money. It's gone now. I might have to take you up on the offer, Mr. Blake."

"Good," replied the tall man.

Holly made her way to the smoldering fire. Tossing a few sticks in the smoke, she made a casual remark about heating some water to wash the dishes. Matt Blake noticed that each wagon contained two large wooden water barrels. McClain and his henchmen had taken a good deal of food, but there appeared to be plenty enough to see the two of them to Tucson.

While the golden-haired lady busied herself, the sheriff sauntered to the grave site. Picking up the shovel, he stepped into the partially dug grave. He had been digging about five minutes when he heard Holly's voice.

"Are you up to that?"

Turning around, he smiled. Sweat bathed his face. His knees buckled.

"Guess not."

Slowly he sat down on the edge of the grave.

"That bullet almost got you," Holly said in a serious tone. "There was bone showing."

"The little skinny jackal with the yellow hair did it. Holey moley! I haven't even told you what I'm doing out here."

"Let's go back in the shade by the wagon and you can tell me," said Holly Lind. "Then you're going to rest."

Making themselves comfortable, the two desert weary travelers sat down in the shade. A slight breeze was sifting through the hollow. It felt good.

A long-tailed lizard watched from a hot rock while Matt Blake told Holly Lind the story of Duke McClain and the events of the last several days.

Holly wiped tears as she heard of Gray Wolf. Blake marveled that she could be so tender after all that life and circumstance had heaped upon her. She had plenty of reason to be bitter. Many women hardened themselves in this raw country. Sometimes it was the only way to cope with the hardships. This was no ordinary woman. There was a marvelous blending of grit and grace in her. She would be at home in a king's palace, he thought. Or she would be a sturdy asset to a hard-working dirt farmer in a log cabin on the prairie. In fact, this woman would have the wherewithal even to be married to a... *That breeze sure feels good.*

"Why don't you put your head down and rest?" Holly said, making a command sound like a request.

Matt Blake reminded himself that he had almost forgotten about women's subtle ways. How long had it been? Twelve years.

It was nearly dark when the Arizona lawman awakened. Lifting his head, he looked around for Holly. Not in sight.

Standing up, he took in the last rays of the sunset. There was a vast bank of shimmering yellow, shot with purple streamers.

Casting his gaze through the trees, he saw three graves. There was the golden-haired lady, standing in the third. Dirt was shooting out, a clump at a time. As the tall man approached the clearing, she said, "How about a lift, Mr. Blake?" She raised her hand toward him.

"Sure, Mrs. Lind," he said, extending his hand.

"You may call me Holly," she said.

"If you'll call me Matt," he retorted with a smile.

For a brief moment he held her hand. Then he turned it up. In the fading light he could see the raw blisters. He reached down and lifted her other hand. Wincing, she withdrew them.

"Not too many shovels in a kitchen," she said.

"I'll bury them for you, ma'am," Blake said.

"How about after I feed you a good meal? You'll have more strength, then. I have a lantern."

"Fine," said Blake, his eyes full of admiration for this gallant woman.

Darkness claimed the desert as a delicious meal was devoured by two hungry people. While Holly washed dishes by the campfire, the bright moon lifted itself into the sky, a silvery ball of light. When she had finished, Blake said, "I don't think you will need the lantern, ma'am. That moon is almost bright as day."

The tall man stood beside Holly in the moonlight. Quietly she wept over the three mounds of dirt. Tilting the Bible to catch the moon's rays, she read aloud. It sounded to

Matt like she was quoting rather than reading.

As they approached the campsite, Holly said, "Now it's bath time. You can go first, Sheriff. Sorry you can't wash your hair. I'll put a new bandage on it, though, after you've bathed."

As Matt Blake bathed in the moonlight behind the same boulder where Holly had stood watching Duke McClain murder three elderly people, she rummaged through some boxes in the wagons.

"Mr. Blake, here's one of Pa's shirts," she said from the other side of the boulder. "It may be a little tight in the shoulders, but it's better than that tattered shirt you've been wearing."

"Mr. Blake was my father, Holly," he answered with a touch of sarcasm in his voice. "My name's Matt."

"Thank you," she replied with a chuckle.

About twenty minutes later, the tall man walked into the campsite, a towel dangling from his neck. The badge on the front of his clean shirt glistened in the moonlight. Holly watched as he put his vest on over the shirt. He picked up his black belt and empty holster where he had dropped them.

"Feel better now?" Holly asked with a smile.

"Much."

Holly Lind disappeared behind the boulder with a fresh bucket of water. Wearily, Matt Blake buckled his gun belt, tied the holster to his leg, and wished for his gun.

Sitting on the ground, he leaned back on the wagon wheel. Holly had kindled a fire. The aroma of hot coffee roused him.

Later, as Holly emerged into the campsite, Matt Blake looked at her over a steaming cup of coffee. She was drying her hair with a towel.

"The air is getting cool," she said. "Got this done just in time." Moving close to the fire, she began to brush her hair.

The sheriff sipped his coffee and watched her in silence.

"You haven't told me about yourself, Mr. Matt," she said, breaking the silence.

"Not much to tell."

"Are—are you married?" She attempted to keep a casual tone in her voice.

"Was."

"Oh?"

"She died."

"Oh, I-I'm sorry."

"Don't be," he said. "It was twelve years ago. She died giving birth to our first child. He died too."

Holly Lind studied Blake's features in the combined light of the full moon and the flickering fire. Somehow she had felt there was no wife waiting for the tall man. There was a haunting atmosphere of loneliness about him.

Sensing she had touched a tender spot, Holly veered the questioning in another direction.

"Are you from this part of the country originally?"

"I guess you'd say that. Born in Santa Fe. My father was town marshal. He was gunned down by a band of outlaws when I was nineteen. Pa had taught me how to draw and shoot. I went after them. They split up. Two of them went to El Paso. I trailed them. Shot it out. Trailed the other four to Tucson.

"Town was pretty small then. They terrorized the people. Killed the sheriff and took over the town. I was so filled with vengeance, I had no fear."

The brush was making a cracking noise in Holly's hair. Little sparks appeared in flashes of green and white. Matt Blake noticed that her hair was as beautiful in the moonlight as in the sunlight. Maybe more so.

"I caught two of them at the livery stable," he continued. "Shot it out. Caught a slug in the leg. The two that were left came at me from the street. By the time they were laying dead in the street, I had another bullet in the same leg and one in the shoulder.

"Time I was healed up, Tucson had a new sheriff and the people wanted me as deputy. I haven't talked like this to a woman since...since..."

"Don't apologize, Matt," Holly smiled. "I asked the question. I really did want to know."

Pinning her hair into place, she said, "Now, we'll get that bandage changed."

Matt Blake was feeling a little dizzy as he lay his head on the makeshift pillow Holly had devised for him. Handling the wound for a fresh bandage had left it throbbing with pain.

"You get some sleep, now," she said, tucking the blanket around his neck.

"We'll head for the Tank tomorrow," he said sleepily.

Matt Blake smelled breakfast cooking before he opened his eyes. As he stood and stretched, a broad blaze of yellow was now flaring in the east and long slender clouds of bright gold and pale red were adorning the morning sky.

Next to the crackling fire was a pan of hot water. Holly was climbing out of the far wagon. As her feet touched the ground, she saw the tall man. His face broke into a broad grin as their eyes met. It crossed Holly's mind how white and even his teeth were.

"Feel better?" she asked with interest.

"Feel great," he said. "Get a little breakfast in me, I can wrestle a grizzly bear."

Extending a shaving cup, speared with brush and razor, she said, "Why don't you use these, so I will be able to tell which one is the bear. You can use that hot water," she advised, pointing toward the fire.

Blake rubbed his stubbled face with the tips of his fingers. "Maybe if I leave it on I could brush that old grizzly to death with it," the tall man said with a twinkle in his eye.

"Breakfast will be ready when you're finished," she replied, quickly turning toward the fire.

By midmorning, Matt Blake and Holly Lind had loaded the wagons and hitched up the teams. George Lind's horse wore a halter which was tied to the back of Holly's wagon. Blake's wagon took the lead. Holly followed far enough behind to allow Blake's dust to settle ahead of her.

Matt Blake remembered that this land leading toward Tapanic Tank was heavily spotted with thick patches of paloverde and mesquite. Apparently there was an abundant supply of underground water which found its outlet at Tapanic Tank.

At just about noon, the sheriff's creaking wagon topped a gentle rise, revealing Tapanic Tank in the distance. Pulling on the reins, he waited until Holly pulled abreast on his left side.

"There it is," he said, pointing. One of the horses whinnied. Another followed suit, tossing its head and making the metal pieces of harness give off a tinkling sound.

He knew the horses sensed something. Then the sheriff saw them. A band of Indians was riding from the Tank, straight for them. A little cry escaped Holly's lips.

"They've seen us. No sense running." His eyes squinted against the desert's glare. Blake said, "Apaches, Holly. A dozen…no, more like fifteen. Looks like Hondo."

A deep frown cut across Matt Blake's brow. He was thinking of the atrocities through which Apaches put white women.

"Holly. Listen to me," Blake said, helping her out of the wagon. "Have you got a butcher knife?"

Her face was ashen. "Yes."

"Get it, quick. Hide it somewhere on your person."

"It's in a box in your wagon," she said, walking toward Blake's wagon. He lifted her into it, noticing how his arms were once again feeling a measure of strength. He was glad. Those two arms may be my only chance, he thought.

Once more on the ground, she put the knife under her blouse on the side. With fearful eyes, she looked up into the tall man's somber face.

"We've only got one chance," he said. "I am going to work on Hondo's pride. Indians are a proud people. I will challenge him to a knife fight. My father was one of the best.

He killed five of the Apaches' best in knife fights. He taught me. I've killed two. Hondo must be the third."

Holly's lips quivered. "Oh, Matt," she said with a trembling voice, "you're in no condition to fight anybody. You've lost a lot of blood." Her fingers dug into his muscular arms. "You're too weak. He will kill you!"

"It's the only chance we've got," he said. "Now, Holly. Listen to me. I'll get Hondo to give his word that we go free if I win. His men will stand by it. Indians despise the white man because he breaks his word.

"If—if he kills me…" He swallowed hard. "You point that knife toward your heart and fall on it."

A cry escaped from her lips. "Matt, I don't think I could do it! I…"

"You must! I have seen what Apaches do to white women. It's indescribable. Promise me, Holly. Promise me!"

Her lips tight, she nodded her head. Suddenly she was in his arms. He held her close, trying to squeeze courage into her trembling frame.

The hooves of the Apaches' horses were drumming thunder into Matt Blake's ears. Lifting his eyes, he saw Hondo astride the big zebra dun. One thing was evident. Hondo had caught up with Duke McClain and his two friends.

CHAPTER TEN

The Apache band brought their horses to a halt, lifting a cloud of dust. Their bronzed bodies glistened in the desert sun.

Matt Blake recognized the butt of his revolver protruding from Hondo's wristband. His Winchester was in the saddle boot. One of the bucks was wearing Duke McClain's hat. Two others were wearing Chamberlain's and Nichols' hats.

Hondo spoke a sharp command in Apache. Quickly, the entire band dismounted and surrounded the wagons. The Apache leader smiled as he approached Matt and Holly. Her fingernails dug into Blake's arm. He could feel her trembling.

Studying Blake's bandage, Hondo said, "White eyes lawman almost lose scalp?" Throwing back his head with a bellowing laugh, he said, "Hondo will finish job!"

The sheriff knew he must act quickly. "Hondo is not man enough to take my scalp by himself!"

Hondo's laughter was swallowed by the hot desert air. His face grew dim. His eyes narrowed. Beating his fist against his chest, he shouted, "Hondo more man than white eyes!"

"I offer you the chance to prove it," Blake said in a monotone.

One of the Apaches pulled a knife and started toward the sheriff.

"No!" Hondo barked, motioning the Indian back with sharp gestures. With a grunt, the buck backstepped.

"Hondo cannot fight wounded man," the Apache leader said. "Would be great dishonor."

"But it would be an honor to kill me with the help of your friends when I am wounded and unarmed?" Blake clenched his teeth. "Hondo is a yellow-bellied coward!"

The Indian's eyes widened. Anger clouded his face. He shook his fists. "Hondo no coward!"

"Then prove it!" Blake said. "Meet me man to man with knives."

The Apaches began to talk among themselves. Holly Lind stood close to the tall man, scarcely breathing. Hondo's eyes followed the circle of red men as they talked in their native language. Matt Blake understood enough Apache to know that the bucks were casting some doubt on Hondo's courage. The sheriff's plan was working perfectly. Hondo's position of leadership, along with his pride, was hanging in the balance.

Through narrowed lips, he said, "You have your fight, white man."

"There are some conditions that go with it," Blake retorted. "I want your word that if I kill you, the lady and I ride away unmolested."

Hondo spoke in Apache toward the circle of red men. Each one nodded his head. "You have my word, white eyes," he said.

"I also want my horse and my guns," said Blake.

Again the Indian spoke to the band. They nodded. Hondo slipped the Colt .45 from his waist and laid it on the seat of Blake's wagon. Barking another command, he motioned toward the wagons. The bucks nearest the horses hitched to the wagon led them out of the circle.

Matt Blake looked down at Holly. Her face was ashen. Her lips were quivering. He said, "Go climb in your wagon." Laying her head on his chest, she clung to him tightly. He held her in his arms for a brief moment. A flash of an unnamed something swept over him. Suddenly he knew that he must win. He must win for her sake. A shadowed chamber in his heart that had been sealed for twelve years burst open.

Without looking back, Holly ran through the circled line of Apaches and climbed onto the seat of her wagon. One of the bucks stepped to the front and held the horses. Slowly, the golden-haired lady turned and looked at the tall man.

Matt Blake untied the rawhide string around his thigh. Unbuckling his gunbelt, he let the empty holster fall to the ground. "Got a knife I can borrow?" he asked, looking Hondo straight in the eye.

Hondo called one of the bucks by name and barked a command. The designated Indian pulled his knife and, throwing it end over end, stuck it half the blade length into the ground, not an inch from Blake's booted foot.

As the tall man stooped over to retrieve it, Hondo let out a war whoop and sprung at him, knife swinging. Matt Blake sidestepped as the Indian rolled in the dust. With fury in his eyes, he charged Blake again.

As he came in, Blake chopped him with a left hook, as hard as he could swing. It caught Hondo square on the jaw and sent him reeling backward. The impact of the punch shook Blake all the way to his knees and he almost lost his balance. His head began to throb. One thing for sure—he must kill the Indian quickly. The loss of blood had taken its toll on his strength.

Hondo staggered to his feet, shaking his head. Blake lunged toward him, aiming the knife at the red man's throat. Hondo swung downward and Blake's knife whistled harmlessly through the hot desert air.

The Apaches were cheering Hondo on. Knives flashed in the sunlight as the men jabbed and circled each other. Once, Matt caught a glimpse of Holly. Her eyes were fastened on him.

Hondo yelled and charged again, throwing himself on Blake's legs. Blake went down, almost on top of Hondo, but the agile Apache rolled free and pounced on top of the lawman. Hondo's knife was raised to strike. In a brief flash, Matt thought of Holly. He arched his body violently, pitching Hondo up and slightly to one side. The knife came down, but Blake twisted out of the way and it buried itself in the sand.

Blake's head was pounding as he scrambled to his feet. Hondo, yanking the knife from the sand, charged again. Blake let him rise to full kneeling height, then slammed a knee beneath Hondo's chin. The Indian's teeth clicked together. He sagged backward and stretched out full length. Blake, winded, took that moment to suck in air. Hondo rolled and came up, spitting blood from a bitten tongue.

Charging again, the Apache came with full force. The tall man sidestepped and came around with the knife in a full arc. Hondo yelled and Blake felt something warm spray on his hand. There was a deep gash in the Indian's shoulder. Blood was flowing profusely.

Like a wounded beast, he charged Blake again. Their bodies collided and they sprawled in the dust. Blake's head struck the ground and light exploded before his eyes. In the nick of time, he rolled away from the swishing blade of Hondo's knife.

The Indian was on top of him again. Hondo grasped Blake's wrist, pinning his knife hand to the ground. The lawman reached upward with his free hand, squeezing his fingers around the wrist that held Hondo's knife.

For several seconds, neither man could move his knife hand. It seemed to both like an eternity. Blood was running down Hondo's arm. Matt Blake could feel blood flowing from his head. The wound had opened when his head hit the ground. In that moment which seemed like an eternity, he thought again of Holly. He thought of what the Apaches would do to her if he died. He thought of that strange unnamed feeling that came over him when he held her close to him.

Hondo's breath was hot in Blake's face. Murder was in his eyes. There was a sudden, almost superhuman strength in Blake. Arching his body, he flung the Apache over his head. As Hondo rolled, fighting to regain his feet, Matt was on him, knife swinging. The blade plunged full length into the Indian's side, under his left arm. He fell backward, dropping his knife. Blood began to gurgle in his throat as he screamed with pain. The sheriff knew that the knife had punctured the lung. Death would be slow.

As Hondo writhed on the blood-spattered ground, the knife still in his side, Blake picked up the Indian's own knife and plunged it through his heart. He let out one last cry...and died.

Matt Blake stood over Hondo's lifeless form, gasping for breath. His broad shoulders lifted and dropped in unison with his heavy breathing. He could hear Holly sobbing as she ran up behind him. Wrapping her arms around him, she wet his shirt with tears.

Not a word was spoken by the Apaches. Silently, they hoisted the body of their fallen leader to the back of a pinto. Without looking back, they rode away, dejected and forlorn.

As the tall man held Holly Lind in his arms, his lungs ceased begging for air. Soon the only sound was from Holly. Her sobbing had subsided into a steady whimper.

"Go ahead, Holly, cry it all out," he said. "Everything will be all right now."

Blake thought of Duke McClain. No doubt he would find the outlaw's mangled body, along with those of his friends. He wondered what twisted reason fate could have in denying him the pleasure of putting a rope around the heartless killer's neck. Certainly McClain had died a horrid death at the hands of the Apaches, but he should have had to face the judge and jury. His crimes were against white men. He should have been executed by white men.

The dun nickered, tossing his head. The sudden sound

invaded his thoughts, bringing him back to the moment. Through her tears, Holly was saying, "Oh, Matt, your head is bleeding badly. Come over to the wagon and let me put a clean bandage on it."

Nearly an hour had passed when the two wagons, each trailed by a horse, moved toward Tapanic Tank. Holly trailed Matt by some fifty yards, allowing his dust to settle ahead of her. Periodically, the sheriff turned his bandaged head to check on the golden-haired lady.

She had never known a man like him. Sometimes when he towered over her, he seemed like a formidable giant. He was a powerful man…both in physique and in spirit. Yet she saw in him a gentleness that was virtually unknown in this raw and rugged country. His steel-blue eyes flashed with violence and death as he fought for his life…and hers. Yet those same eyes softened into pools of tenderness when he had looked into her frightened face and held her close.

The sun was commencing a westward drop in the afternoon sky when the wagons approached Tapanic Tank. It was a grim and lonely place, surrounded by tall desert cactus, mesquite shrubs, and scattered rabbit brush. Two huge bald-faced boulders formed a sort of gateway, where a trail led into a giant formation of rocks.

Matt Blake pulled his wagon to a halt just in front of the two boulders. He climbed out of the wagon and waited for Holly. As she reined the horses to a stop, he approached her wagon and helped her to the ground.

"You wait here," he said. "I saw some buzzards dive behind those rocks awhile back. I'm pretty sure what I'm going to find in there." Holly nodded.

As Blake walked toward the natural gateway to the Tank, he noted how good it felt to have the Colt back in his holster. He felt balanced now.

Rounding the boulders and stepping into the shade of the tall rocks, his eyes fell first on the spring of cool, clear water. Several buzzards screeched at this surprise appearance and their giant wings set up a roar as they fluttered toward the sky. There were the white naked bodies of two men, streaked with blood.

The one nearest his was lying face down. Blake booted him over. As he saw the bloody mass, his blood ran cold. He was not sure whether it was Chamberlain or Nichols. His scalp had been taken, leaving a meaty horror where his hair had been. The skin of his face, loosened by the scalp's removal, had sagged downward. There was no way to identify him.

Blake stepped toward the other man, who was lying naked on his side. His scalp was gone too. The sand was soaked with pools of blood. The tall man felt his stomach growing queasy. The buzzards had been working on what was left of this man's face.

He ran to the spring and splashed water on his face. Holly's voice fell on his ears.

"Matt! Are you all right?"

"Yes! Don't come in here!"

Looking back at the bodies, he decided the first man was Chamberlain. He remembered that he had big, thick hands. Yes. That one is Chamberlain. The other is Nichols. Both were too large to be Duke McClain. McClain! Where's McClain!

Matt Blake scanned the rest of the Tank. Nothing.

Running between the boulders, he approached the wagons.

"Matt. What is it? You're as pale as can be. Are you all right?" Holly took hold of his hand.

"Chamberlain and Nichols. Scalped. Horrible. Buzzards haven't helped it any."

"I saw them come out of there when you went in," she said. "Can I get you something?"

"No thanks," he said. "I'll be all right. McClain isn't in there, Holly." Slipping his hand gently from hers, he began to walk away from the Tank, scanning the sky.

"What are you looking for?" Holly asked.

"The buzzards. If McClain's body is somewhere else, they will be feasting on it, too."

Suddenly the tall man stopped. Lowering his line of vision from the sky to the desert floor, he shaded his eyes, squinting against the midafternoon sun.

"He's out there!" he said, pointing. "You wait here." Blake could see a form lying on a small mound. The buzzards were circling, but as yet, none had landed. Was it possible that Duke was still alive?

The tall man loped toward the motionless figure lying on the mound some four hundred yards away. As he drew nearer, the situation became clear—the outlaw was staked out on an anthill.

McClain had tried to kill Samanti at Indian Head Spring.

Hondo and his men would feel greater animosity toward him than toward Chamberlain and Nichols. The latter would die simply because they were white men. They would die reasonably fast. But the man who showed a great hatred for Indians would die a tortuous, slow, and agonizing death.

The Apaches would lay a man naked on an anthill face up and stretch his arms and legs full length. Stakes would be driven deep into the earth next to the wrists and ankles. Then they would bind the wrists and ankles to the stakes with wet strands of rawhide. As the rawhide began to dry, it would shrink, binding the victim tighter and cutting into the flesh. The ants would begin to swarm over the body of the intruder of their domain. As long as the victim remained motionless, the little insects generally would not bite. But soon the rawhide would begin to cut. The burning sun would blister tender skin. The awful sensation of the crawling insects would become unbearable. All of this combined with the knowledge that there was no escape would send the victims into spasms, screaming with terror.

If the Indians wanted to hasten the death of their captive, they would spread a thin film of honey over his body. As the ants bit into the honey, they would also bite the skin. The combined poison of thousands of bites would kill the victim within four or five hours.

Without the honey, the victim's life span would depend on how long he could lie there without moving. Once he began to move, he would infuriate the ants and they would bite him violently.

As Matt Blake approached the mound, he saw the naked

body of Duke McClain stretched out on the anthill. Thousands of red ants were swarming over him. His eyes were closed, but the sheriff could see him breathing. A warm flow of joy pulsed through him, just to know that his prisoner was still alive.

He stepped to the top of the mound. Duke's lips were held in a tight line to keep the ants from crawling into his mouth. His unsteady breathing made a whistling sound as it passed through his nose.

Matt Blake could hear the flapping wings of the buzzard overhead. There was no honey on the outlaw. Probably because Hondo had none. Duke's clothing lay in a heap beside him, covered with ants. They were moving in and out of his empty boots by the score.

Holding his voice to a near-whisper, Blake said, "Duke, don't move. I'm going to get you out of there."

McClain opened his eyes. Blake read the shock and surprise in them.

"Yeah, it's me," he said with a tone of irony.

The outlaw blinked against the ants crawling into his eyes. He wanted to speak, but did not dare open his mouth.

"You've held still this long, just do it a little longer. I'll be back in a few minutes."

McClain blinked his eyes in acknowledgment and then held them tightly closed. For a brief moment, the sheriff studied the scene. McClain's wrists and ankles were bleeding, but not too badly yet. His fair skin was sunburned, but he would recover.

Blake figured that Hondo must have staked out McClain

after he killed his partners and was just coming from doing so when he and Holly met him. McClain had been there a little over three hours.

Spinning on his heels, he bolted into a dead run for the wagons. He was breathing hard when Holly met him some fifty yards from the wagons.

"He's still alive," Blake said between gasps. "I've got to figure a way to get the ants off him before I cut him loose. Any sudden moves and they'll bite him to death."

"After what I saw him do to Ma and Pa Lind and Uncle Jake, I would like to say leave him there…but I can't. Can I help?"

"Maybe you can. There's still plenty of water in the barrels. If I can douse him with a lot of water real fast, maybe I can keep them from biting him. C'mon. Let's get in my wagon."

While the wagon sped toward the anthill, Blake explained his plan to Holly. He would carry both barrels and set them down just above the outlaw's head. With both lids removed, he would dump one barrel on McClain from his head downward, washing the ants toward his feet.

If they started biting before Holly could hand him a bucketful of water dipped from the second barrel, it would be only his feet and legs that would be bitten. The second dousing should clear them from his feet and legs and give Blake time to cut the rawhide.

As he pulled the wagon to a halt, a cloud of dust sifted upward. Quickly, Blake had a barrel on his shoulder, carrying it up the mound.

Holly gasped. "Matt Blake! You didn't tell me he was naked!"

"Shhh! You'll frighten the ants!" he said with a semiwhispered chuckle. "Sorry. I never thought to tell you!"

Returning for the second barrel, he stuck Holly's butcher knife under his belt and hoisted the barrel onto his shoulder.

"Got the bucket?"

"Uh-huh."

"Let's go."

As he set the second barrel down, he noticed McClain blinking his eyes. Holly was at his heels.

"Close your eyes, Duke. I'm going to douse you with this barrel, then with a bucket. As soon as I cut you loose, you jump and run. All right?"

The outlaw blinked his eyes. Blake lifted both lids and laid them down quietly. Holly dipped and filled her bucket, trying to look away from the outlaw.

The tall man hoisted the first barrel and the water struck Duke McClain with a whooshing sound. Quickly the bucket was emptied toward his feet. The stunned insects floundered in the water as Matt Blake moved from stake to stake cutting rawhide cords.

McClain, yelling at the top of his lungs, scrambled to his feet and ran behind the wagon, swatting at several remaining ants.

Holly began to stomp her feet and brush at her skirt when she suddenly became aware that the ants had taken a liking to her.

Matt Blake was shaking McClain's clothing as he walked

around the wagon toward the sunburned outlaw.

"As soon as I can get the ants out of your pants, you can put them on, Duke," he said, laughing.

The outlaw was watching Holly, while doing his best to cover himself behind the wagon. The tall man flung the wad of clothing in McClain's face, saying, "I'll get your boots."

As Blake picked up McClain's boots, turning them upside down and beating them together, he caught Holly's eye. She was trying to melt him with flashes of green fire.

He could not hold back the grin that forced itself on his lips as he said, "Really. His being naked just didn't cross my mind! Besides…he seems to be more embarrassed about it than you are. Look how red his face is!"

The charm of this tall, handsome man was more than she could resist. The corners of her mouth turned upward, her lips parted revealing beautiful white teeth, and she laughed.

It struck the tall man that he had not seen her laugh before. For a moment, he could not decide under which emotion she was the most beautiful…anger or delight. Either way, he thought, she has got to be the most beautiful woman alive.

The sun was dipping its flames below the western horizon as Matt Blake shoveled the last dirt on the common grave of Rob Chamberlain and Will Nichols.

As he returned to the campsite beside Tapanic Tank, the smell of food cooking reminded Sheriff Matt Blake how long it had been since he had eaten. Holly was bending over the fire as he pitched the shovel into a wagon.

"Hungry, Matt?" she said with a warm smile.

"Like a bear," he said, glancing toward Duke McClain.

The outlaw was stretched on his back, unable to maintain a sitting position. Periodically, he lifted the front of his shirt from his sunburned chest. Blake approached, standing over him.

"How did you do it, lawman?" McClain asked in an even tone.

"Do what?"

"Come back from the dead."

"Didn't. You just thought you killed me."

A deep frown clouded the outlaw's brow. "I shot you in the head! I saw the bullet hole!"

McClain winced as his shirt pressed against his sunburned chest.

"You were so drunk," Blake continued, "you couldn't have told a bullet hole from an ink spot."

"You'd just better be thankful that I was drunk, mister, or I'd have blown your head off!"

"You're the one that ought to be thankful, little man," said Blake.

"Whaddya mean?" McClain asked with a curled lip.

"If you had blown my head off, you would've died on that anthill. It wouldn't have been bad until you couldn't hold still any longer. Then those ants would have bitten you to death. The Apaches know that is a horrible, slow death. The noose in Tucson will be a lot faster."

McClain said nothing.

"Hey!" Holly's voice broke the silence. "Dinner's ready!"

"Let's eat, Duke," the sheriff said, jerking his head toward the fire.

Slowly the outlaw rolled to his knees, cussing the pain. Clambering painfully to his feet, he let out a wail. He had not put on his socks or boots. It was bad enough with his shirt and pants touching his tender skin.

Bent over like an old man, he hobbled to the place where the golden-haired lady had arranged plates, silverware, and cups. Holly ignored him.

"Sit down, Duke," Blake said with a false tone of friendliness. It was obvious that a sitting position would be excruciating.

"I'll stand," the suffering outlaw said.

While Holly ate slowly, staring into the fire, Matt Blake set the outlaw's plate and cup in the back of the wagon so he could stand to eat. McClain chomped his food and slurped his coffee like a starved animal.

Darkness had enveloped the land when the trio had devoured the meal. Matt and Holly sat near the fire.

The sunburned outlaw stood crouching at the tail of the wagon, supporting himself with one hand.

"Where'd you run into this here woman, Blake?" McClain asked with genuine interest.

"She's not just a woman, mister," Blake snapped. "She is a lady. And don't you forget it." The sheriff's eyes looked black against the light of the fire. Holly turned her gaze toward Blake and studied him for a long moment. Other than her father, she had not known a man to watch over her so carefully.

"You don't recognize these wagons?" Blake asked with a sharp, bitter tone.

The outlaw studied them in the dim light. Suddenly it came to him. He looked hard at Holly. "B-but where…"

"She was hiding behind a boulder among the trees. Saw you murder her in-laws."

McClain's face blanched.

"Too bad we can't hang you for those murders, too. Got a sure 'nuff eyewitness. She won't be needed, though. We've got plenty of eyewitnesses to hang you for killing Margie Kendall."

The tall lawman smiled. "Dead man's noose. Isn't that what you said, Duke?"

McClain's eyes looked weak in the flickering light. He fought to hold his face expressionless. Matt Blake saw through the mask. The outlaw was frightened at the mere thought of the noose.

Night sounds enveloped the campsite as conversation dwindled. Holly Lind could hear both men breathing evenly. She heard the sound of little desert creatures scurrying about. A cluster of clouds covered the moon. Soon the curtains of slumber closed around her.

The pain of the sunburn gave Duke McClain a restless night. With each move, hot daggers of pain stabbed him awake. Just before dawn, he finally slept soundly.

A strange spectral hand seemed to pull him through a clouded mist into a place where the dawn was breaking on the eastern horizon. In the dim light, he could see the horrible outline of a crude gallows silhouetted against the gray sky. Opening his mouth, he tried to scream. Nothing would come out.

Thoughts raced through his mind. "I'm going through this awful thing again!"

Stiffening his weakened legs, he dug his heels into the dirt. Again, something strong was forcing him toward the gallows.

The terrified outlaw tried to cry out. His voice refused. Sweat was pouring down his face in spite of the morning breeze. Wiping the stinging moisture from his eyes, he blinked against the first rays of the sun as they illuminated the crowd of people gathered at the base of the gallows.

Their eyes! He tried to scream. The sightless white pools sent cold chills up and down his spine. The ranchers and their families were there as before, beckoning him to his execution. People he had gunned down on the streets, the bank employees, and Margie Kendall…empty white pools where their eyes should be. Margie was screaming as before, "Murderer! Murderer! Murderer!"

Suddenly, there were some faces in the crowd which had not appeared the first time he went through this. It was the elderly couple, George Lind and his wife. Next to them was Jake Lind. Their sightless eyes seemed to pierce his soul.

A strong arm behind him was forcing him up the steps. He could not catch a glimpse of the face behind him. Midway up the steps, he paused to look down. The crowd mocked him with hollow laughter. Oh, those horrible white pools!

There, again, was the young rancher's wife. He was trying to find her husband's face in the crowd, when the strong arm at his back hurried him upward. As he reached the platform, he looked down at the trap door. The laughter of the crowd thundered in his ears.

He was pushed onto the trap door and spun around. He was looking into Matt Blake's face. Blake's eyes were normal. He hadn't died!

The words formed in McClain's mind, though they refused to leave his mouth. "You're dead! I shot you! I saw the bullet in your head!" Blake began to laugh.

Something brushed McClain's head. Lifting his eyes, he saw the dreaded noose swaying in the breeze. Again, he tried to cry out. Nothing. The sheriff held the black hood in his hand. "I promised you this noose, McClain, and I keep my promises," Blake said in a half-whisper.

As the hood dropped over his head, everything went black. The sheriff was slapping the outlaw's face with short, stinging blows. "Wake up!"

Duke McClain opened his eyes. They were wild.

"Hey, man, you were having some kind of a nightmare," said Blake.

The sky was gray with light. The sun was about to usher in a new day. McClain sat up and looked around. Holly was standing beside the fire, looking coldly at the outlaw.

"Yeah…some kind of nightmare," McClain said.

By the time breakfast was ready, the tall man had shaved and combed his hair. The outlaw ate standing up at the wagon. After Holly had placed a clean bandage on Matt Blake's head, the trio pulled away from Tapanic Tank with water barrels and canteens full.

As the dust lifted from the wagon wheels, Matt Blake

looked at the outlaw sitting next to him, then glanced at the sun. "We need to put half the distance between us and Diago Springs behind us today," he said. Glancing behind, he could see the sunlight shining on Holly's hair, between dust clouds.

Shaking his head as he straightened in the seat, he was aware once again of the strange sensation in his breast. Thoughts began darting through his mind. "Can I be falling in love with her?" He had fallen in love with Jeannie casually and progressively. They had known each other for over a year before they had become serious.

"I've only known Holly for a few days," he told himself. "Must just be that I have been so long without female companionship. Besides, a lovely lady like that deserves a real chance at life. Especially after what she's been through. Sure wouldn't be right to tie her down to the hardships of a lawman's wife."

"Jeannie did it, but she loved me mighty powerful." He shook his head. "What am I saying, anyhow? Holly couldn't love a desert rat like me. She needs to go east and find her a polished gentleman. Got to get this kind of thinking out of my head."

Out of the corner of his eye, Blake saw Duke fall from the wagon seat. Pulling back on the reins, he stopped the wagon. The outlaw was lying in a heap on the ground.

"Duke, what's the matter?" the sheriff asked as he knelt beside him.

"Dunno," he muttered. "I just got dizzy and fell off the wagon."

Holly's wagon halted beside the two men, sending up a

mass of dust. "What is it, Matt?" she asked.

"He's got a fever. Felt dizzy and fell off the wagon," the tall man replied. "Maybe you'd better take a look at him."

Holly did not reply. Neither did she move from the wagon. She was thinking of what McClain had done to the Linds.

"Holly. You coming?"

"Yes," she said without emotion.

Kneeling beside the sheriff, she looked at the flushed face of the outlaw. His body began to shake. His teeth were chattering. Blake had not tied his hands because of the wounds left by the rawhide cords. Besides, McClain could not yet stand to wear his boots over his socks, so he would not be running anywhere.

"Matt, look," said Holly. "His feet are swollen something awful." Pushing his pant legs upward, she pulled off his socks. His calves, ankles, and feet were nearly twice their normal size.

"Holey moley!" gasped the sheriff. "Could the sun have done that?"

Before the golden-haired lady could answer, Duke said, "It's the ant bites." He swallowed hard. "I didn't t-tell you. When the Apaches first l-laid me on the anthill, I s-started squirmin'. A whole lot of 'em b-bit the backside of me. I learned q-quick, when I quit squirmin', they quit bitin'!"

Matt unbuckled Duke's belt and yanked his pants off. Holly gasped, turning away.

"It's all right, he's covered. Look at this!" the tall man said. Slowly she turned and looked.

"Aggggh!" she said, turning away. From the thighs down, McClain was covered with large red spots. His thighs were also badly swollen.

Looking back, she said, "Matt, he's full of poison from the bites. No wonder he didn't put his boots on. He couldn't have gotten them over his feet."

"What should we do?" the sheriff asked, looking into her emerald eyes.

Holly stood up, staring at the outlaw. The cold-blooded murders she had witnessed were fresh in her mind. McClain avoided her icy stare. He knew what she was thinking.

"I'm sick, Sh-Sheriff," McClain chattered. "Y-you gotta h-help me!"

Holly stared for a long moment. Hardly parting her lips, she said, "We had better go back to the Tank. We will have to get him as cool as possible. Depends how much poison is in him whether he will live or not."

By noon, Duke McClain lay up to his neck in the shallow pool of Tapanic Tank. The cool water helped to hold his fever in check.

While the golden-haired lady knelt beside the pool, splashing water on Duke's fevered brow, Matt Blake watered and tethered the horses.

As the blazing sun bent toward the western sky, the tall man approached the pool.

"How's he doing?" he asked, standing over Holly.

"I'm not sure. He's a mighty sick man."

"We've got to pull him through."

Holly chuckled. "Sort of ironic, isn't it?"

"We've got to keep him alive so they can hang him."

"That's justice," he replied.

"I'm not too sure he's going to make it, Matt," Holly said. "I don't know what to do, but try to keep him from burning up and hope he can wear out the poison."

The sheriff studied the outlaw's face. "He's in bad shape all right. Somehow he's got to make it. I promised him a noose. I aim to keep my promise."

The hours passed until the sun kissed the western horizon and bid the desert good night. The golden-haired lady and the tall man ate supper beside the pool. The ailing outlaw seemed to worsen with the coming of darkness.

Taking turns during the night, the weary pair watched over Duke McClain. The long night finally gave way to the day.

During the day, McClain's fevered brain went into delirium. He spoke with thickened tongue of going to the gallows. He cried something that neither Holly nor Matt could understand. Something about eyes. At times, he clawed at his neck, as if he were trying to tear away the noose.

At sundown, the fever broke. Now, it appeared, he would live. It would be several days before he could travel.

CHAPTER ELEVEN

A s Pete Clendon turned the key in the lock, he looked up the street to see Wiley Chance coming from the sheriff's office. The deputy waved with an "I want to see you" gesture.

The Western Union agent nodded and waved back. Turning the knob, he stepped into the telegraph office, leaving the door open behind him. The clock on the wall indicated the time was two minutes after eight o'clock.

Pete Clendon was a small, slender man in his early sixties. He had operated the telegraph office in Tucson since the day it opened eighteen years ago. He was slipping the visor cap on his head as the young deputy stepped through the door.

Glancing at the clock, Wiley Chance smiled as he said, "Say, Peter, you're two minutes late openin' up shop. You're liable to get yourself fired!"

A twinkle flashed in Clendon's eye as he retorted, "I don't tell you what time to go to work, sonny, you don't bother tellin' me!"

"Well, you old codger, I jist might write a letter to Mr. Western Union and say,

DEAR MR. UNION, YOU HAVE GOT THE LAZI-
EST OLD SCALAWAG IN ARIZONA WORKIN' IN
YOUR OFFICE HERE. TRUTH IS, HE AIN'T
WORKIN' AT ALL. HE OPENS UP AT ELEVEN
FORTY-FIVE IN THE MORNIN' AND CLOSES FOR
LUNCH AT NOON. HE OPENS AT THREE O'CLOCK
AND CLOSES AT THREE-FIFTEEN!

"How would you like that, huh?" said Chance, poking a finger into Clendon's meatless rib cage.

"You do that and when Matthew Blake gits back, I'll tell him you took off and went fishin' soon's he clumb on that there stage fer Yuma!"

"Why, you old coot, that'd be lyin'!" Wiley Chance said with his eyebrows arched and his lower lip stuck out.

"Wal, yer letter to Mr. Union wouldn't be no affidavit you'd want to swear on in court, neither!" snapped Pete Clendon.

The two friends laughed together. Pete looked at Wiley's handsome face and said, "Speakin' of the sheriff…ain't he 'bout due?"

"That's what I wanted to talk to you about. I figger some-thin's happened to Mr. Blake. It's been nine days since he wired us from Yuma that he and 'Mad-dog' McClain were leavin' the next mornin'. Seven oughtta be enough."

"What'd you want me to do?" Pete asked, with a worried tone.

"Send a wire to Sheriff Hankins and ask him if Mr. Blake

and McClain left on schedule. Ask him if he's heard anything since they left."

"Okay. I'll let you know soon's I git an answer," Peter replied.

"Thanks, Pete," Wiley said, turning toward the door.

"Say, Wiley…"

"Yeah, Pete?"

"Don't you git all up in a stew, now. Matthew Blake can take care o'hisself!"

"Yeah. You just let me know when you hear from Hankins."

Wiley Chance stepped out on the boardwalk and headed toward the sheriff's office. Pete Clendon listened as the jangle of Chance's spurs slowly faded away.

Hal Stedman was seated behind Sheriff Matt Blake's desk as Wiley Chance came through the door.

"Well?" said Stedman.

"Pete's gonna let us know soon's he hears from Sheriff Hankins."

"And if Mr. Blake left on schedule, we're gonna go lookin' for him, ain't we?"

"Yep. Let's go git some breakfast."

The two deputies crossed the street to the Honey Dew Café. They presented a sharp contrast to the eye. Chance was tall and slender, Stedman was short and stocky. Both were students of Matt Blake. Hence, good with their fists and fast with their guns.

Sheriff Matt Blake and Holly Lind turned their wagons northeastward just after sunrise on the third day after Duke McClain's fever subsided. McClain lay on his back in the bed of Blake's wagon, weakened from his ordeal.

Holly followed at her usual distance, avoiding the dust from the lead wagon. The zebra dun followed Blake, George Lind's bay followed Holly.

The land between Tapanic Tank and Diago Spring was dotted with giant saguaros and squat cacti. Mesquite shrubs flourished amid the rocks and shallow arroyos. Greasewood was seen in patches across the desert floor.

The heat was upon them almost from the moment the sun rose. It built with each minute until by noon the sand and granite that surrounded them gleamed with the sun's intensity. The temperature had edged over a hundred degrees. It was as if they were riding through a giant oven, in which they would bake until the sun went down.

Matt Blake stopped his wagon in the thin shadow of a butte where a few stunted cedars grew amid a ragged stand of greasewood, Holly pulled alongside.

They remained there for a while, giving the horses a little water and treating themselves to a small quantity. The outlaw received a more generous portion. The savage fever had dehydrated him.

Blake noticed that Duke had not shown any of his meanness since the stakeout on the anthill. He wondered how he would behave as he started feeling better, especially as they drew nearer to Tucson.

Capping the canteen after taking his own portion, the sheriff said to Holly, "Wish we didn't have to be so stingy with this, but if Diago is dry, we've got to go all the way to Tucson with what we have."

Holly smiled. "We'll make it, Matt."

The sunshine accented a little dimple in her left cheek when she smiled. He silently scolded himself for not having noticed it before. "You'll have to be more observant from now on," he told himself.

Once again the wagons were rolling, dust rising. The tall man remembered that the halfway point between Tapanic Rock and Diago Spring was a rockbound canyonlike section which lay hard against a giant monumental rock formation. He was determined to keep moving until they reached it. They must reach Diago Spring by tomorrow night. Then they would have just a day and a half to Tucson.

It suddenly struck the lawman that he had lost track of the days. He did not even know what day it was, much less the date. "It's still got to be August," he told himself. "I sure couldn't tell anyone the date."

The afternoon lumbered by, with two more stops for water. Sundown came after an eternity of burning punishment. They pulled through the brief canyon and made camp at the base of the giant monument.

Matt Blake tethered the horses while Holly Lind prepared supper. Just before darkness fell, he climbed a high rock, had a thorough look at the bleached, shadowed desert around, saw no sign of danger, and returned to the camp.

Duke McClain was hobbling around the camp, trying to limber his stiffened body. Holly pretended to concentrate on her culinary duties, but warily watched the outlaw out of the corner of her eye.

"How's the food holding out?" asked the tall man, approaching the fire.

"If we should have to go longer than three more days, we'll be in trouble," Holly replied.

"Barring Indian trouble, we should make it in two and a half," said Blake. "Haven't seen a sign of a redskin since the Tank."

"I hope we don't, either," she said.

A cool breeze began to blow, scattering smoke in little swirls and raising a cluster of sparks from the fire.

With the dishes washed and Duke already abed in the wagon, the weary travelers walked together in the moonlight. The cool breeze raised little goose bumps on their skin. The camp lay about sixty yards behind them. They were still close enough to detect any unnecessary movement by the outlaw.

Holly looked up at the tall man towering over her. The moonlight accentuated the silver tips of his temples, in sharp contrast to his dark leathered face. The silver in his moustache seemed to add a touch of dignity to this big gentle man.

"How strikingly handsome he is!" she told herself.

"Sure is quiet at night, isn't it?" Blake said.

"Mmm-hmm."

"Moon sure is bright."

"Mmm-hmm. Sure am glad to see you without that bandage on your head. The wound is hardly noticeable now."

"I had a good doctor," he said, smiling.

"He has the most even and perfect teeth I've ever seen," she told herself.

"Is it all right if I stay at your house till I can wire my sister and make arrangements to go to Denver?"

"Sure is," he said.

"I just hate to put you out of your home."

"No problem. I can sleep just as good at the office."

A gust of wind swept past them, lifting Holly's golden hair. When it settled back, a small ringlet fell on her forehead. The tall man gently reached down and put it back in place. He saw the moon reflected in her eyes. Another gust of wind dropped the ringlet back on her forehead. A smile tugged at the corners of her mouth.

Chilled by the wind, she began rubbing her arms briskly. "You're getting cold," he said with concern in his voice.

"Wish I could store some up for tomorrow," she said with a full smile.

Squinting his eyes, he studied her face. "Can't see it now," he said.

"Can't see what?"

"Your little dimple."

"Oh…that," she said, dropping her face.

"I hadn't noticed it till today when the sun hit it just right."

She did not reply. Slowly she stepped toward him, tilting her head back. His powerful arms closed around her. Closing her eyes, she gave him her lips.

Matt Blake awakened to the sound of pans and dishes rattling. The aroma of breakfast cooking filled his nostrils. Opening his eyes, he saw that the sky was overcast. Holly was busy laying out silverware and plates.

Looking at him in the gray light of dawn, she smiled and said, "Breakfast is almost ready. You'll have to shave after we eat. I'll keep water hot for you."

Without speaking, the tall man smiled and stood to his feet. Yawning, he stretched full length, then scratched his ribs.

"You want to wake up the yellow-haired one?" she asked in a flat tone. Matt figured she would boil McClain in oil if she had the chance. Neither could he blame her. He had to admit he had the same feelings. If he weren't a lawman, sworn to uphold the law, he would have killed McClain the first time the little man stepped out of line. He would've liked to have left him on the anthill. It would have served him right. But now Blake knew he would have the satisfaction of putting the noose around his neck.

"Wake up, Duke!" the sheriff shouted. The outlaw jumped, shook his head, and groaned. "Get out of the wagon. It's time to eat."

Holly and Matt were already eating when the stiff-legged little man approached the fire.

"There it is. Help yourself," Matt said.

The outlaw wolfed down his breakfast without saying a word.

"You're looking better, Duke," Blake said.

"Uh-huh."

The outlaw was thinking to himself, "In another day or so, I'll be strong enough to make my play, Mr. Lawman."

Black clouds were hanging low as the wagons moved out toward Diago Spring. Duke McClain was lying in the back of Blake's wagon, feigning weakness, but gathering strength.

From time to time, Blake glanced behind him, checking on Holly and observing McClain. With the sounds of rhythmic hoof beats and squeaking harness filling his ears, along with those of the creaking wagon, his mind returned to the events of the night before.

The beautiful Holly, small and slender, felt perfect in his arms. He thought of how her lips were like crushed velvet. Her emerald eyes were indescribable when filled with moonlight. He remembered the almost holy silence of the desert after he kissed her. Neither spoke a word as they turned and walked together back to the campsite. It was as though both they and the desert knew that any sound would mar the beauty of that ecstatic moment.

Looking back through the dust, he saw Holly smile. He was glad for her sake that the sun was obscured. The breeze that carried the dust southward was almost cool.

Lightning flashed on the eastern horizon. The thunder rumbled like distant cannons.

"Holly Lind, you have no business letting that tall handsome man fall in love with you," she told herself. "What if he does, and should ask you to marry him? You could not give him children. A normal man wants children. You had best curtail any more scenes like the one last night."

There was no doubt in Holly's own heart. She had fallen in love with Matthew Blake. She wanted him more than anything she had ever wanted in her entire life. Her love for Hank Lind had developed more or less into a brother-sister type relationship even before they were married. She had loved Hank, but not with the kind of love that was burning in her heart for the tall man from Tucson.

She saw in Matt Blake a magnificent blend of strength and gentleness. When he had to be tough, he was tough. There was a strength in his arms when he held her last night…but a touch of tenderness revealed that he felt as if she were a little glass doll.

Hank Lind had never shown gentleness or tenderness toward her. He was often rude and rough. When he started drinking, he became mean. With Lind she felt like a bond servant and sometimes like a piece of furniture. Matt Blake put her on a pedestal. To him she was a lady. She was someone to be loved and cherished.

A bolt of lightening overhead interrupted Holly's thoughts. It was so close, the crack was ear-splitting. Suddenly the horses reared. Matt Blake pulled his team to a halt and twisted in the seat to look at Holly. McClain sat up. The thunder boomed and Holly's team bolted. With all her strength, she pulled back on the reins.

Blake bounded out of his wagon. The frightened horses paused with the sudden pain of the bits and then bolted again. Holly saw Blake running head-on toward the team. She yanked the reins again. The team paused, biting at their bits. The second pause gave the tall man just the break he needed to charge between the horses and grasp the inside reins.

"Whoa! Whoa, boys!" he shouted. Immediately the fright was over. Holly could hear him talking gently to the animals. Jumping from the wagon, she ran into his arms.

"Holly, darling…are you all right?" The "darling" had slipped out, but he did not care. She should just as well know it now.

"Oh, Matt! You could have been killed!" she said with tear-filled eyes. "They could have trampled you to death!"

"If they had gone to a full run, that wagon would have struck a rock or a hole and turned over. I couldn't let anything happen to you."

She laid her head on his chest. He could feel her trembling. "It's all right now, darling. We'll stop here for a while."

After an hour's rest, the wagons were rolling again. A gentle rain was falling. It was a welcome contrast to the heat they had endured the past several days.

By the time they had reached Diago Spring, the rain had stopped and the clouds were breaking up. It was almost dark.

Diago Spring was situated in a shallow arroyo, encircled on all sides by mounds of sand and odd-shaped boulders of various sizes. Mesquite was thick, along with cactus and galleta grass. The spring was yielding water. Matt Blake was relieved to know that they could head for Tucson the next day with a full supply of water.

By the time supper was over, the stars were twinkling in the heavens and the moon turned the white desert sand to a glistening silver.

Diago Spring was surrounded with scattered bones and

skulls of men and beasts. Over the years, many had come to the spring in search of water and found it dry. Unable to go on, they laid down and died. The sight of the skulls in the moonlight made Holly Lind shudder. She did her best to ignore them.

After Duke had fallen asleep in the wagon, Holly and Matt sat beside the fire and watched it slowly die out. Somewhere in the distance a wild beast roared. Almost instantly another beast roared in answer. Holly scooted closer to the tall man. He smiled, putting his arm around her. The rain had put an extra chill in the night air. The warmth of his big frame felt good.

How safe and secure she felt in this big man's presence. There was an air of confidence and raw power about Matt Blake. The golden-haired lady thought how wonderful it would be to spend the rest of her life with this rugged man of the desert. Then a sudden pang of sorrow raked across her heart. This could never be. Matt Blake deserved a wife who could give him a family.

Slowly he released her and, moving back a little, took her shoulders in his hands. "Holly…I just as well should come out with it. I love you."

She started to say something. He placed the tip of his finger on her lips. "Please let me finish," he said.

"I didn't recognize it at first, but now I know. I flat fell in love with you the moment I opened my eyes and saw you looking down on me. You may say that it is just infatuation stimulated by the desert and the moonlight."

He swallowed hard.

"Holly, I'm no infatuated school boy. I'm a forty-one-year old man. For twelve years I have been very lonely. I've met a lot of women. Some of them have been very fine ladies. But I never saw one that deserved a second glance.

"I've tried to drown and suppress my loneliness by staying involved in my work. I had pretty well resolved in my mind that this would be my lot for the rest of my life."

Holly felt her heart pounding in her breast. She could feel the throbbing in her temples.

"Then I found you," he was saying. "I know that you belong back east somewhere. You belong in a beautiful house with fine furniture and tapestry and crystal chandeliers. You are a real, genuine lady."

The tall man swallowed hard again. "On the other hand," he continued with a slight quiver in his voice, "you have the makings to handle the raw life of this western frontier. You have displayed rugged courage and character which is rarely found in a woman who has retained her femininity."

Holly could see the love in his eyes. Her mind was swirling. It would be unfair for Matt Blake to be tied to a woman who could not give him children.

"Holly, darling. I love you." Like melted wax, she folded into his arms. He kissed her with tender fire. Her fingers pressed tight on the back of his head. He kissed her repeatedly until her breath was gone.

When his hands released her shoulders, she sprang to her feet, turned, and ran toward a large boulder. He stood and watched her as she stopped and leaned her head against the boulder.

Slowly he approached her. Her face was bent downward. Placing the tips of his fingers under her chin, he tilted her face upward. The light of the moon revealed tear-streams.

"Holly…I…I'm sorry if I said something wrong. I didn't mean to hurt you or upset you."

She lifted her hand to stroke his leathered cheek. "You haven't hurt me," she said. Her lower lip quivered as she tried to speak. The lump in her throat hindered her voice.

How could she tell him she loved him, but could never let herself be his?

"Holly. I…I am asking you to become my wife," the tall man said with emotion. Her eyes met his. The tears continued to wash her cheeks.

"I know I have no right to ask you to live the hard life of a lawman's wife. But I would be good to you. We would be happy together. I think I could make you love me in time…"

"Oh, Matt," she sobbed. "I do love you, my darling. I do love you!"

Bending over, he wrapped his arms around her small frame then straightened up. Her feet dangled. Her breath was warm in his ear. When she spoke, tiny fingers danced on his spine.

"I love you more than I could ever tell you. We've known each other only a few days, but I feel that I've known you all my life."

Squeezing her gently, he said, "Then you will marry me?" Silence prevailed.

"Holly…"

"Oh, Matt. I want to say yes…but…but…"

"But what?"

"I-I don't know if it would be right."

"You mean to marry a man who wears a badge?"

"No. It's not that. It isn't what you are. The problem lies with me."

Gently he lowered her to the ground. "What is it, Holly? Is it something I don't know about?"

"No, Matt. Not really. It's just that…that…"

She looked into his eyes. Again she stroked his cheek. "I need a little time. Time to think things through. Would you give me a little time?"

"I guess knowing a fellow a few days is just a little short for such a big decision. Sure. I understand."

"Thank you," she said. "If loving you was all there was to it, I would marry you the minute we reach Tucson. It's just that…that…"

"It's all right," he said with a tone of assurance. "You don't have to explain. You take your time and I'll ask you again in five minutes!"

Holly laughed. "You big ape!" Reaching up, she pulled his head down and kissed him tenderly.

Morning came with a flourish of orange fire in the eastern horizon. Matt Blake was shaving when Holly began to stir. The fire crackled and the coffee pot danced over the flame.

"Good morning," he said.

She sat up and stretched. "Good morning. Sorry I'm so lazy. I laid awake for quite awhile."

Bending over with lathered face, Matt smiled and said, "Is there ever a time when you're not beautiful?"

"Oh, Matthew," she said, blushing.

Duke McClain arose and for the first time since the stake-out, put on his boots. Sitting by the fire, he ran his fingers over his stubbled face.

Holly was busy preparing breakfast over the fire. Blake was standing some thirty feet away, adjusting the knot on the leather cord that held the holster to his thigh.

Turning her head from side to side, she said, "Matt, have you seen the butcher knife?"

The sheriff looked up just as McClain sprang to his feet, wrapped his left arm around Holly's neck, and standing behind her, held the butcher knife to her throat. A gasp escaped her lips.

"All right, Sheriff! I want that gun. Reach down and lift it slowly out of the holster and lay it on the wagon seat. Go on! Or I'll cut her lovely throat!"

Slowly, Matt Blake lowered his hand to the butt of the Colt .45.

"Take it by the fingertips!" McClain shouted.

With ease and determination, he put his full hand on the gun butt and lifting it upward, extended his arm full length. The muzzle was pointing straight at the outlaw's head. As he raised his left hand to steady his wrist, he thumbed back the hammer.

"Blake, I'll kill 'er!" McClain screamed.

"If I let you get your hands on this gun, you'll murder both of us. Drop the knife or I'll blow your head off," Blake hissed through clenched teeth.

"You might hit her, mister. You know that, don't you?"

"I can blow the right eye out of a rattlesnake at fifty paces, McClain. You lower that knife nice and easy or I'll splatter what little brains you've got all over the desert."

Holly looked at Matt. In all her life, she had never seen such fury in a man's eyes. There was a dark and terrible look on his face. Something tugged at her senses. Something tightened inside her stomach. His steel-blue eyes seemed to flash fire. A muscle in his left cheek twitched. She could almost hear his teeth grinding inside his mouth. His hands held the big .45 steady.

The outlaw's breath was putrid in her nostrils. He was breathing in short gasps.

"I'll cut her, Blake! I swear I will!"

"I'm telling you one more time. Lower that knife right now."

"You won't shoot me," McClain said between gasps. "You want to hang me too bad! A noose is no good for a dead man, remember?"

"I'll forfeit the noose for her sake," said Blake.

The outlaw read the message in the lawman's eyes.

He lowered the knife from Holly's throat.

"Hand it to her, Duke. Handle first," Blake commanded.

The little man obeyed. Holly stepped away from him and ran to Blake. The fury in the lawman's eyes seemed to freeze McClain in his tracks.

Blake eased the hammer down and handed the gun to Holly, butt first. Dropping his arms to his sides, he walked toward McClain, opening and closing his fists. With clenched teeth, he looked down at the frightened outlaw and said, "You've done your best to kill me and I've tolerated it and gotten angry. But you put your filthy hands on the lady. This time you've made me mad."

McClain began to back up, lifting his palms toward the furious lawman, as if to hold him at bay. "I'll report you, Blake! This is brutality on a prisoner! You'll lose your job! Th-they'll take away your b-badge!" The outlaw's back was now against a boulder. His beady eyes widened as Blake reached under his vest and pulled out the badge. Tossing it aside, he said, "I'm taking a leave of absence. Now I'm just Matthew Blake, private citizen."

The cornered killer swung a fist at the tall man, which went wild. A left jab popped his head back and a hard right hook caught his jaw on the rebound. McClain bounced off the boulder and fell flat on his face.

Blake picked him up, braced him against the boulder, and with a well-aimed punch, hit him square in the mouth. Duke's knees buckled and he collapsed in a heap. Holly started to cry out as Blake picked him up again. He had regained his temper and was merely carrying the unconscious McClain to the wagon.

When the outlaw regained consciousness, he was bound hand and foot, lying in the back of the wagon. As he sat up, facing backward, Diago Spring was already out of sight. The sun was midway in the morning sky.

He rolled his tongue around the inside of his swollen mouth. His front teeth were missing. Twisting around to look at Matt Blake, he found the sheriff eyeing him.

"Good morning, Duke. Did you sleep well?" Blake said with a false tone of friendliness.

McClain's eyes were filled with fire as he glared at the law-man. Turning back around, he dropped his aching head to its original place.

Blake looked back at Holly. She blew him a kiss. Facing forward again, he pondered her request for time to consider his proposal. Certainly theirs had been a short relationship. Much different than with Jeannie. He would just have to give Holly time. He did not like to think about what he would do if she refused to marry him. He assured himself that it would turn out all right. She loved him. In the final analysis, that was all that mattered.

The sun was at its high point in the sky when Matt Blake decided it was time for rest and water. There was nothing immediately ahead which offered any shade. They would just have to tolerate the sun.

Suddenly he saw them. Three riders and a wagon were dead ahead, coming straight toward them. Blake pulled the wagon to a halt. Holly pulled her wagon alongside.

"Stopping for water?" she asked.

"More than that. Riders coming our way."

Duke McClain raised up on his knees and squinted against the sun.

The sheriff had alighted from the wagon. Walking around to the far side of Holly's wagon, he lifted his rifle from the saddle, which lay in the bed. Cocking a cartridge into the chamber, he handed it to Holly. "You ever use one of these?" he asked, with concern written on his face.

Holly nodded.

"You drop back to your usual spot. If trouble starts, you do what's necessary. Savvy?"

"Uh-huh," she replied, her face grim.

"Hyah!" shouted Blake. The wagon lurched forward, jerking McClain to his back. A vile oath escaped his swollen lips.

With narrowed eyes, the lawman watched the approaching riders. They were no more than half a mile away now.

All of a sudden, as they drew closer, Blake recognized Wiley Chance's big black gelding. Only one black horse had a blaze like that. He squinted hard, trying to focus on its rider. Sure enough. It was his deputy. The excited sheriff stood up and began waving his dirty gray Stetson. The big black horse broke into a gallop. Chance was coming strong, waving his own hat.

Blake stopped the wagon, leaped to the ground and bounded forward. Holly watched with interest as she saw the rider of the black horse swing from the saddle. The two men wrapped a bear hug on each other, then stood face-to-face beating each other on the back.

Seeing that everything was all right, she pulled her wagon alongside of Blake's. The tall man turned around and smiled. "Holly! It's my deputy, Wiley Chance! Wiley, this is Holly Lind!"

The golden-haired lady nodded. "Pleased to meet you, Mr. Chance."

"Likewise, I'm sure, ma'am," said Chance, lifting his hat.

Looking past Wiley at the approaching men, Blake said,

"Who you got with you, kid?"

"Well, there's George Gilbert, Derl Fox, and Randy Bowman there on the water wagon."

"What are you blokes doing out here?" Matt Blake asked with a smile.

"Lookin' fer you."

"Yeah?"

"Yeah. When it got past time for you to be pullin' in, we wired Sheriff Hankins to make sure you left when you said you would. He wired back that you had and he hadn't seen hide nor hair of you since. So, we lit a shuck after you."

"I really appreciate that, Wiley," the tall man said with sincerity.

"We'da been on you sooner, but we had to take a detour and dodge a band of Apaches."

Gilbert, Fox, and Bowman halted their horses, shouting in unison, "Howdy, Sheriff!"

"Howdy, boys!" Blake countered with a wave. After shaking each man's hand, he introduced them to the golden-haired lady.

Wiley Chance was studying the yellow-haired outlaw, who was now sitting uncomfortably in the bed of Blake's wagon. "I see you have 'Mad-dog' in tow, Mr. Blake," he said. The other men laughed.

Chance stepped a little closer, eyeing McClain's puffy face. His left eye was now swollen nearly shut and encircled in deep purple. "What happened to you, McClain...," he said, "run head-on into a stampede?"

The outlaw scowled at the deputy, but said nothing.

"Where did you find this lovely lady?" Chance asked Blake. "Did you run into any Indians? What slowed you down? How—?"

"Wait a minute! Hold fire!" interjected Blake. "Let's get the horses and everybody watered. Then we can get moving toward home. I'll have one of the boys here drive Holly's wagon. You can ride on the seat with Holly and me and we'll tell you the whole story."

Including a night's rest, they were just about a day's ride from Tucson. As the horses and wagons lifted dust, Duke McClain cursed the ropes on his wrists and ankles. All hope for his escape had now passed into oblivion. His neck was as good as in the noose.

CHAPTER TWELVE

Tucson's main street lay in a true line east and west. Its thirteen hundred residents lived in an area five blocks in length and eight blocks in width. Main Street ran right through the middle, five blocks long, with four streets on either side.

The three central blocks on Main Street housed the business district. The rest were taken up with two churches and several houses, along with a few vacant lots.

Entering Tucson from the west, one first confronted Main Street, with nine houses and five vacant lots on the left, eight houses, four vacant lots, and the Baptist church on the right.

The next block began the business district, with the Golden West Hotel on the left, followed by the Bluebird Café, Hank Dixon's Gun Shop, Caldwell's General Store, Myrtle Heller's Dress Shop, Dr. John Sander's office, and then the office of Alexander Haddock, Attorney-at-Law.

Directly across the street from the Golden West Hotel was the livery stable, Sam Ketchum, proprietor. Next was Gosney Feed and Grain, followed by the Shamrock Saloon, Clayton Wright's Undertaking Parlor and Wagon Works, two vacant lots, and the Arizona Drug and Sundries on the corner.

Diagonally across from the drugstore in the next block was the Mountain View Hotel. Next to the hotel was the Western Union office, followed by a vacant lot, the Arcade Tonsorial Parlor, the Red Coyote Saloon where Margie Kendall was shot, the B. & L. Café, and another vacant lot.

Directly across the street from the Mountain View Hotel was Lyon's Gun and Hardware. Next was the Stillman Coach Lines and Stage Depot, followed by the blacksmith shop, Harris Mercantile, two vacant lots, and the sheriff's office and County Jail.

The next block housed the county courthouse, two more saloons, Maude's Café, a men's clothing store, the Tucson Gazette, and several other businesses interspersed with vacant lots.

The following block revealed the Methodist church, two vacant lots and eight houses on the left, and twelve houses and two vacant lots on the right. Sheriff Matt Blake's house was the third one from the west corner, on the right.

The desert-weary party headed by Sheriff Blake pulled into Tucson just before two o'clock in the afternoon. Holly sat beside the tall man on the wagon seat. Duke McClain was sitting up in the back of Blake's wagon, leaning against a water barrel. His wrists and ankles were still tied.

Derl Fox drove Holly's wagon. As the procession made its way slowly forward, a group of boys playing in a vacant lot spied the sheriff.

"Hey look, fellas!" an older boy shouted. "It's Sheriff Blake…and he's got 'Mad-dog' McClain!"

A clamor arose as the boys started shouting and running

ahead of the procession, proclaiming the news. Dogs were barking. A woman stepped out the front door of her house, wiping her hands on a soiled apron. An old man called from his front yard, "Howdy, Matt!" Blake nodded.

People were staring from the windows of the Golden West Hotel. A group of cowboys loitering in front of the Shamrock Saloon stopped their conversation and gawked. Horses standing at hitching rails swished their tails at the pesky flies.

Hank Dixon stood in the door of his gun shop and waved. The din was growing louder as more children, dogs, and adults joined the procession.

Reverend Paxley, the Methodist minister, was standing on the boardwalk talking with Clayton Wright. Both men looked up and waved. "God bless you, Matt, you brought 'im in, didn't you!" Paxley said with feeling.

Duke McClain scowled at the minister.

Curious eyes peered from the windows of the Mountain View Hotel, while several men waved from the hotel's porch. Pete Clendon came running out of the telegraph office. Jogging alongside the sheriff's wagon, he shouted, "I'll wire the U.S. Marshall in Denver and let him know, all right, Sheriff?"

Matt Blake nodded and smiled.

Harry Mashburn, the barber, and a customer stood on the boardwalk, staring. The customer had shaving cream dripping from his face.

As the wagon veered to the right, toward the sheriff's office, Duke McClain's eyes fell on the Red Coyote Saloon.

This was where he'd played the fool and shot the dance-hall girl in front of a whole crowd. McClain cursed under his breath.

As the wagons pulled to a stop, Deputy Hal Stedman emerged from the sheriff's office, showing his mouthful of white teeth.

Shaking hands with the sheriff, he exclaimed, "Boy, I sure am glad to see ya, Mr. Blake!"

"Got accommodations for Mr. McClain, here?" asked Blake, nodding toward the sullen outlaw.

"Shore do!" replied Stedman. "We've had a room reserved jist for him for a long time!"

Turning toward Holly, who still sat in the wagon, Matt said, "Hal, I want you to meet Holly Lind."

"My pleasure, ma'am," said Stedman with a broad grin as he removed his hat.

"Pleased to meet you," Holly replied.

"Hal, make up my bunk here at the office, will you?" asked Blake. "Mrs. Lind is going to occupy my house for a few days. I'll be sleeping here at the office."

"Yes, sir!" answered Hal Stedman.

"I'll take her to the house and get her situated. Then I'll be back. You and Wiley take McClain and lock him up!"

"With pleasure!" Stedman said with a smile. Together, the two deputies lifted Duke McClain out of the wagon.

Matt Blake shook the reins and clucked at the horses. The wagon lurched forward. In less than a minute the wagon halted in front of a white house surrounded by a picket fence.

"Matt, your house is lovely!" Holly exclaimed.

"Not to press an issue, but it can be your house, if you want," he said with a half-smile.

She started to speak when she heard a door slam. From the house next door, a small boy of about five years of age came running toward them. As Matt stepped down from the wagon, the lad shouted, "Sheriff Mister Blake! Sheriff Mister Blake!"

"Hi, Bobby!" the tall man shouted, extending his hands.

Holly watched with mixed emotions as Matt took the boy up in his arms. The tall man's eyes sparkled like midnight stars as he and the boy laughed together.

"I sure did miss you, Sheriff Mister Blake!" Bobby said.

"I missed you, too, Bobby!" the tall man said. "Bobby, I want you to meet someone." Lifting him onto the seat beside the golden-haired lady, he said, "Bobby, this is Mrs. Lind. Mrs. Lind, this is Bobby Mitchell."

"Hello, Bobby," she said with a smile.

"Hello," he answered. "Is she going to stay at your house, Sheriff Mister Blake?"

"Yes, she is," Blake answered.

"She sure is pretty. Is she going to stay at your house a long time, Sheriff Mister Blake?"

Matt looked into Holly's eyes. "I sure hope so, Bobby," he said.

Holly tried to hide the turmoil going on inside of her. In her thoughts for the last few hours, she had begun to weaken. She had been telling herself that possibly she could marry Matt in spite of her barren womb. Certainly he remembered that she could not bear children. He left no doubt that he wanted her for his wife.

In this moment, as she saw Matt with Bobby, an icy hand seemed to squeeze her heart. This kind and gentle man should have a son.

It seemed Holly's turn to speak. She parted her lips, searching for words, when she was spared by a woman's voice.

"Bobby!" It was Bobby's mother approaching the wagon. "Bobby! Mr. Blake has things to do. Now you come on home."

The boy stood up in the wagon.

"We're so glad you're home safe and sound, Sheriff. I hope Bobby didn't get in the way. He just idolizes you. You're the only man in Tucson he wants to be around since his daddy died."

"He's no problem, Katie. We've got a lot of special things between us." Motioning toward Holly, he said, "Katie Mitchell, this is Holly Lind."

Both ladies smiled and greeted each other.

"Holly is going to be your neighbor, Katie…"

The flash of disappointment in Katie Mitchell's eyes did not go unnoticed by Holly Lind.

"Oh," Katie said, trying to disguise her feelings.

"…for a few days," Matt said, completing his sentence.

"Oh?" Katie said in a lighter tone.

"I'll be staying at the office," he interjected.

Holly did a quick study of the situation. Katie Mitchell was a widow with a little boy who adored Matt Blake. Matt Blake was a widower who had lost his only son. It was also evident how he felt about the boy. It was just as evident how Katie felt about the tall man. Holly could see it all over her face.

Katie was a very attractive lady. Holly sized her up as being about five feet five and around 120 pounds. "That would put her about two inches taller and fifteen pounds heavier than me," she mused.

Katie's hair was coal black. She had a nice figure and a pleasant personality. Holly guessed that she was about twenty-nine or thirty. "Two or three years younger than myself," she mused again.

The two women eyed each other for a brief moment.

"Nice to meet you, Miss Lind," Katie said, taking Bobby by the hand.

"Likewise, I'm sure," said Holly. Holly figured the "Miss" had gone unnoticed by Matt and she was too tired to correct it, so she let it go.

"Bye, Sheriff Mister Blake," said Bobby.

Holly opened the windows of the hot, stuffy house, while Matt carried her things in from the wagon.

"This place needs a woman's touch," Holly said, straightening pictures on the walls and adjusting the knick-knacks.

Matt Blake slipped up behind her, folding her into his arms. "I wholeheartedly agree," he said.

Turning around in his arms, she laid her head on his chest and wrapped her arms around him.

"Have you made up your mind yet?" he asked with caution.

The icy hand squeezed her heart again. Something twisted in her stomach. Leaning back to look at his face, she said, "We'll talk about it tonight. Right now I want to find me some water and take a bath. You need to go to your office, I'm sure."

"The cupboards are well stocked. There's money in a jar in the cabinet over the stove. I'll leave the wagon here in case you need to go to the store. I'll send a man with a barrel of fresh water right away. I'll be here for supper about six-thirty."

Bending down, he kissed her nose, then held her tight as he kissed her lips. Without another word, he turned and started out the door. When he paused and looked at her, he said, "I love you, Miss Lind."

She laughed briefly and with emotion said, "I love you, Sheriff Mister Blake."

At six-thirty on the dot, the tall man approached the door of his house. The team and wagon were still tied where he had left them. He had taken the dun to the livery stable when he left earlier.

A pleasant aroma was coming from within. Sticking his head through the open door, he said, "Holly! All right if I come in?"

When she stepped through the kitchen door into the parlor, his heart leaped and burst into flame. She had fixed her hair in little ringlets, sweeping it upward on the back of her neck and letting the front fall in a wave across her forehead. Her clean dress made a swishing noise as she walked toward him.

His arms tingled as he held her close. She kissed him warmly.

"Hungry, Sheriff Mister Blake?" she asked.

It was dark when Holly and Matt had finished doing the dishes together.

"I've got to take the team to the livery stable. Would you like to ride along?"

"I'd like that," she replied.

Guiding the horses out the east end of town, the tall man said, "I know a short-cut to the livery stable."

A fifteen-minute ride placed them on a ridge at the base of Tucson's mountains. The town lay spread out below them. Lights twinkled yellow in the windows, in contrast to the silver of the moon's rays.

"Thought we could talk up here," Matt said. He stepped from the wagon and, placing his hands on her tiny waist, lowered her to the ground.

"Have you had time to think about it, Holly?"

"Oh, Matt. I'm so confused."

"You mean about loving me?"

"No. No, my darling. That's a settled issue," she answered.

"What is it, then?"

"Well…" She bit her lip.

"Don't be afraid to tell me, honey. I know it's something mighty big. Please tell me."

Clearing her throat, she choked on the first few words.

"It's just that I can't give you a son. I can't give you any children at all."

Her last words trailed into a sob. Gripping her shoulders, he looked into her tear-dimmed eyes.

"Holly, darling, is that what it is?"

She nodded, choking back the sobs. Holding her close, he said, "That doesn't make any difference to me."

"Maybe not now, but it will later," she sobbed.

"But Holly, I love you more than anything in the world. Don't you know that?"

"Yes. Yes, I do…but…" Swallowing hard and struggling to hold her composure, she continued. "But when I saw you with little Bobby today, I knew that I am no good for you."

"Holly, don't talk like that."

"Katie Mitchell is in love with you."

"Katie?"

"Yes."

"Naw, she just likes me because Bobby does."

"Oh, Matt, you men are so…so stupid sometimes! It was written all over her face today."

"I wouldn't trade you for a thousand Katies," he said with conviction.

"But she already has a son. You could become 'Daddy' to him, instead of 'Sheriff Mister Blake.' And she could give you more children."

"I don't love Katie," he said. "I love you."

"But if I went away, you would forget me in time. Then you could find happiness with a wife who could give you children."

"But Holly—"

"Matt, you had one son taken from you. It's only right that you have another chance. I just can't do this to you."

"But if I say it's all right, isn't that enough?"

Shaking her head, she said, "I've just got to be sure I'm doing the right thing for you…for now and for the rest of your life. Matt, I just need more time to think it out."

"I don't understand, but I'll go along with whatever you say. What do you want to do?"

"I would like to go visit my sister in Denver. It would give us both time. Maybe you will feel different about it then."

"Never," he said.

"Will you let me have the time?"

"Of course, my darling, if that's what you need. There's a stage from here to Denver three times a month. Comes from Denver and turns around here. The next one will be September seventh. That's nine days from tomorrow. We can wire your sister in the morning."

Duke McClain's trial was held on Monday, September third. The courthouse was filled to capacity. Hundreds stood outside. It took less than a day. By two-fifteen, the last witness was heard. Judge Daniel B. Peterson finished his speech to the jury by two-thirty. The jury went out. They returned in twelve minutes.

Matt Blake and his deputies sat just behind Duke McClain. As the jury filed in, the outlaw grew tense. He wiped the sweaty palms of his hands on his pants.

"Has the jury reached a verdict?" the judge asked, peering over the top of his half-moon glasses.

Harry Mashburn, owner of the Arcade Tonsorial Parlor, was the foreman. Getting to his feet, he said with a heavy voice, "We have, Your Honor."

"Will the defendant please rise?" asked Judge Peterson, looking at Duke McClain.

The outlaw's chair made a scraping noise on the wooden floor. Matt Blake eyed him as he stood up. He thought of the contrast between how he looked out on the desert with a gun in his hand and how he looked at that moment. All the starch was gone.

The judge looked back at Mashburn. "And how do you find the defendant?"

"Guilty as charged."

Blake could not see McClain's face, but his body did not flinch.

"The defendant will approach the bench," the judge said.

Blake, Stedman, and Chance got to their feet. The sheriff stepped forward and stood a pace behind McClain, just to his left. Blake noticed the little man was trembling.

The judge spoke with a heavy, stern voice. "Mr. McClain, you have been found guilty of first degree murder by due process of law. This court has proven beyond the shadow of any doubt, that on the date heretofore mentioned, you did knowingly and willfully murder Miss Marjorie Kendall in cold blood.

"It therefore becomes my duty to pronounce sentence upon you in the interest of the people of this county. Do you have anything to say before sentence is pronounced?"

Eyes cast to the floor, McClain shook his head.

"What's that?" the judge said with a sharp tone. "I cannot hear you."

"N-no. I have nothing to thay." Duke's four missing teeth caused him to speak with a lisp.

"Then by virtue of the authority invested in me by the people of this county, I hereby sentence you to hang by the neck until dead. Such sentence…"

Duke's knees buckled. Matt Blake caught him before he went down. Steadying him, he nodded to the judge.

"Such sentence is to be carried out by properly designated authorities on Friday next, September seventh." The judge paused, laying his glasses down. Looking the convicted killer straight in the eye, he said, "It is customary to schedule our hangings for sunrise on the day of the execution. However, in your case, I am going to make an exception. Lots of folks aren't up and about by sunrise. I want the whole county to observe your neck in the noose. You will be hung at high noon. May God have mercy on your poor twisted soul."

With the crack of the gavel, the judge barked, "This court is adjourned!"

Friday came especially fast for three people in Tucson: Holly Lind, Matt Blake…and Duke McClain. The Denver stage was due to arrive at ten-thirty that morning and depart at eleven.

At sunrise, Duke McClain sat on his bunk in sullen silence. The sheriff rolled off his cot and stretched his long limbs. Walking stiffly from his office to the cell block in the back, he offered the condemned man anything he wanted for his last breakfast.

Cursing the sheriff, he refused to eat.

Wiley Chance and Hal Stedman came in a few minutes

before eight. "You boys hook up a team and pull the gallows to the usual place," the sheriff commanded. "Go buy a brand new rope. I promised Duke a noose. I want him to have the best."

The gallows was a crude structure, built of solid oak for stability. Standing sixteen feet high at its top, it placed the condemned man's feet some nine feet from the ground as he stood at the trap door built into the platform. This afforded a good view for all. The rope was tied to an eight-by-eight foot beam across the top. It was given enough length to allow the victim to drop through the trap door and dangle beneath the platform. A lever at ground level would be pulled at a signal given by the sheriff, who would stand beside the victim on the platform.

It was built on skids so a team of horses could pull it. Sheriff Blake kept it in an open space behind the jail. When in use, he would place it on Main Street, directly in front of the undertaking parlor. Clayton Wright would be responsible for removing the body and preparing it for burial after Doc Sanders pronounced the victim dead.

Ten o'clock found Matt Blake sitting in a chair watching Holly Lind placing the last-minute things in the two new tan-colored valises he had bought her. Conversation was at a minimum. All that could be said had been said.

At ten-thirty they stepped out the door of the house. Holly looked ravishing in her brand-new blue taffeta dress and blue-plumed hat. They were presents from the tall man with a heavy heart who carried the two tan-colored valises. Peering down the street, he said with a big grin, "The stage isn't there. I hear it went out of business."

"Now, now, Sheriff Mister Blake," she said, laughing, "don't you try to pull one on me!" Her laugh was superficial. Inside, she was full of burning knots.

They were just a few steps from the depot when the stage came thundering down the dusty street behind them. Pulling it to a halt in a cloud of dust, the driver jumped down and pulled open the door. The shotgun man climbed on top and began lowering luggage.

Matt and Holly stood watching as the passengers stepped from the stagecoach. There were two middle-aged women, their husbands, and a teen-aged boy. All whom Matt Blake recognized as citizens of Tucson. The two middle-aged men were carrying copies of the Denver Post. They were asking people if the hanging was going on as scheduled.

The last to step from the stagecoach was a tall, slender man in his late twenties. Matt recognized him as a stranger. The man on top of the coach handed the tall stranger a large valise. In his other hand he carried a small satchel. Matt heard him ask someone where the hanging was going to take place.

In minutes that seemed like seconds to the heavy-hearted couple, a fresh team was hooked to the stage and luggage was being loaded.

Five people stood ready to board, three men and two women. The women were both obese. Very obese. All three men were stout.

Taking her hands in his, the tall man said, "There's going to be an awful lot of flesh on that stagecoach, Holly. It's going to be terribly crowded. Do you really think the trip is worth all that discomfort? Why don't you just stay here and get married?"

The passengers were climbing aboard as the golden-haired lady in the blue taffeta dress kissed the tall man repeatedly. Tears were streaming down her face.

"Oh, Matt, if I only knew you wouldn't stop loving me later because I kept you from having children."

His steel-blue eyes seemed to look into her very soul. With a tone in his voice she had never heard before, he said, "You are all I want. I could never stop loving you!"

"C'mon, lady," the driver was saying, "gotta git this thing rollin'!"

Holly sat down in the small spot they left for her, next to the window. Her tears glistened in the sunlight as the stage spun around and headed eastward out of town. Matt Blake stood with Holly's tears still wet on his face, watching the stage pull away.

As the stagecoach passed the white house with the picket fence, Holly could hear Matt's last words echoing in her mind. The floodgates burst.

Wiley Chance was reading a copy of the Denver Post as Matt Blake entered the office. "This is last Tuesday's paper, Mr. Blake. Apparently the capture of McClain was carried in an earlier edition. The U.S. Marshal in Denver has given the information to the paper. Tells in here all about the judge's speech and the noon-time hangin'."

"Pete Clendon has kept the wires hot about the 'Mad-dog'" replied the sheriff. "Did you boys get the gallows in place?"

"Yes, sir," answered Chance. "Hal's takin' the team back to the stable right now."

"Did you test the mechanism?"

"Yes, sir. We checked the trap door with the sand bag. Everything works perfect. Got a brand-new rope for Duke, too!"

The office door opened. Reverend Lyle Thompson, the Baptist preacher, stepped in. "Morning, Sheriff…Wiley."

"Morning, Preacher," Blake said. "I have my doubts that Duke will see you. C'mon, let's find out."

Thompson was a tall man in his early forties. He was almost as tall as the sheriff. The two men approached Duke's cell.

"Someone to see you, Duke," Blake said.

McClain looked up, squinting his eyes. The left one was still quite purple. He glared at the Bible in Thompson's hand.

"No preachers, Blake," growled McClain. "Git him outta here!"

Thompson stepped forward. "Mr. McClain, I—"

"Git him outta here!" McClain shouted, his face flushing. Quietly the two men returned to the office.

"Sorry, Preacher," Blake said.

The door opened again. It was Reverend Paxley. Entering, he eyed Thompson.

"Forget it, Brother Paxley," Thompson said, "he won't talk to a preacher."

"See you at the hanging, Sheriff," Paxley said with a note

of disappointment. The two ministers left together.

Blake looked at the clock. It indicated eleven thirty-seven. Stepping behind his desk, the sheriff opened a bottom drawer and pulled out a black hood. Folding it over his gun-belt, he glanced out the window. Wagons, buggies, riders, and people afoot were making their way along the street toward the gallows.

Lifting a length of rope from a wall hook, he said, "Let's go tie his hands, Wiley."

At eleven forty-six, Duke McClain emerged from the office, flanked by Blake and Chance. His hands were tied behind his back.

The outlaw began to think of his recurring nightmare. As the three men made their way westward, people along the street stared. Shifting, bulging eyes watched through shop windows.

McClain did not notice them. He was going over the nightmare in his mind. In the nightmare, it was always sunrise as he approached the gallows. The sun was now at its peak in the sky.

As they passed the Mountain View Hotel, a pair of cynical eyes watched the three men from the upstairs corner window. It offered a perfect view of the gallows standing diagonally down the street some two hundred feet.

Passing the drugstore, McClain saw the gallows looming toward the sky. The noose, like a threatening reptile, hung from the cross-beam, swaying in the hot breeze.

The crowd was dense at the base of the gallows. Duke thought of the hollow-eyed accusers who stood in that same spot in his nightmare. He was relieved to see that they were normal, living people.

McClain's tongue felt like a dry rock in the desert sun. His throat was parched. As they stopped a few feet from the gallows, he could hear the sheriff giving last minute instructions to Deputy Stedman, who stood with his hand on a long wooden lever.

The murmur of the crowd had risen to a dull roar. Blake was now saying something to the doctor and to the undertaker, who stood close by. McClain was counting the wooden steps. Thirteen.

Suddenly, the outlaw heard the sharp voice of Matt Blake behind him. "All right. Duke, let's go." McClain stiffened his legs. A strong arm shoved him forward. He heard the word "No!" escape his own lips. Now he was digging his heels into the soft earth. He could not resist the strength of Matt Blake's powerful arms.

As his foot touched the first step, his knees buckled. He was crying, "No! No! No!" as the sheriff carried him up the steps and planted his feet on the trap door.

By this time, the heartless killer who had murdered helpless men, women, and children without mercy was sobbing. The noose brushed against his head. He released a little whimper.

Pulling the hood from under his belt, Blake said, "I promised you this moment, Duke." The trembling little man's eyes were bulging wildly as the hood covered his face.

Matt Blake leaned outward and caught the swaying noose with the tips of his fingers.

Almost simultaneously, the sheriff heard the sharp crack of a rifle and a heavy muffled groan escape McClain's lips. The impact of the bullet sent him hard against the railing. He spun around and fell flat on his back.

Turning toward the sound of the shot, Matt Blake saw blue smoke sifting upward from the upstairs corner window of the hotel. At the same instant he caught a glimpse of sunlight flash from a rifle barrel.

"Wiley! Hal! The hotel. Upstairs corner window!" The two deputies bolted toward the building. The crowd seemed stunned, almost in shock.

"Doc!" shouted Blake. As the physician's boots thumped on the gallows steps, the sheriff knelt down and pulled the hood from McClain's head. His eyes stared sightlessly toward the Arizona sky.

There was a crimson spot on his shirt around a small hole. The bullet had struck him in the heart. Death was instant.

"He's dead, Doc," Blake said.

The doctor took one look. "Sure is," he replied, as he turned and descended the stairs.

A shot rang out in the hotel, followed by three in rapid succession, then one more.

Oblivious to the gunfire, Matt Blake stared down at the corpse. For a moment, he seemed almost in a trance. All the torture of those days in the desert came to mind. He had courted death and suffered heat, all to bring Duke McClain to justice. Duke was supposed to hang. Now someone had deprived justice of its rightful due, with a single bullet.

Wiping sweat from his eyes, he looked down at Clayton

Wright, who stood at the foot of the gallows. "Clayton, take up the slack in this rope. Just wind it tight down there, so it will hang right where it is."

The undertaker complied quickly. Blake tested the rope with a couple of short tugs and knelt down beside the dead outlaw. He started to close the eyes, then checked his hand. "We'll just leave your eyes open, old boy. I want every young man in this town who has any thoughts about following your trade to get a good look at how your kind end up."

Standing up, he wiped his mouth with his sleeve. "I promised you a noose, Mr. McClain," he said, looking into the sightless eyes, "and I keep my promises."

Bending over, he raised the corpse upward and slipped the noose over the head and tightened it around the neck. As he eased the body down, the head tilted to one side.

Descending the steps, he said to Clayton Wright, "I want him to hang there till sundown tomorrow. I want all of Tucson to get a good look at those wild eyes."

Wright nodded.

At that moment, four men approached Clayton Wright, carrying the corpse of the tall, slender stranger who had come in on the stage that morning.

"Take him inside, boys," Wright said. "I'll be there in a minute. It'll be like you say, Matt."

Blake nodded as Wright turned away.

Wiley and Hal gave their report to the sheriff. The man's name was William Spain. Duke McClain had shot down Mrs. Spain during a bank robbery in Burlington, Colorado. Spain was wounded, but recovered. He swore over his wife's grave he would get McClain.

Having moved to Denver, he read of Duke's capture and sentence to hang at noon today. He had to buy off a passenger in Denver to get on the stage.

When the deputies charged his door, he fired at them and they had to shoot him. He lived long enough to tell his short story. Said his life was worthless without his wife. Now he could die happy, knowing he had avenged her death.

"You boys take the rest of the day off," Blake said. "I'll look after the office."

As the tall man started up the street toward his office, he stopped and turned around. The crowd had not yet dispersed. They stood staring at the body dangling from the rope.

He noticed the strange way the sunlight reflected from Duke's eyes. He thought how they looked like empty white pools.

Saying nothing to the people scattered along the street, he made his way toward the office in his usual long strides. As he approached the office, something caught his eye.

Two tan-colored valises were sitting in front of the door. His heart leaped to his throat. Flinging the door open, he saw a golden-haired lady in a blue taffeta dress. Her blue-plumed hat was on the desk.

"We got to the edge of town," she said with a smile, "and I decided there was just too much flesh on that stagecoach. It was terribly crowded. I didn't think the trip would be worth all that discomfort anyway."

She brushed away a tear.

"So I decided to just stay here and get married."